It all begins with a letter.

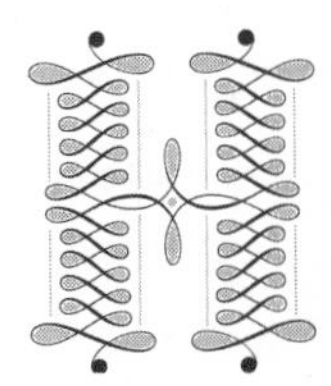

is for Hesse. Penguin Drop Caps is a series of twenty-six collectible hardcover editions of fine works of literature, each featuring on its cover a specially commissioned illustrated letter of the alphabet by type designer Jessica Hische. A collaboration between Jessica Hische and Penguin art director Paul Buckley, whose series design encompasses a rainbow-hued spectrum across all twenty-six books, Penguin Drop Caps debuted with an "A" for Jane Austen's *Pride and Prejudice*, a "B" for Charlotte Brontë's *Jane Eyre*, and a "C" for Willa Cather's *My Ántonia*, and continues with more classics from Penguin.

Penguin Drop Caps is a series inspired by typography—its beauty and its power of expression. A drop cap, or an initial cap, is the first letter of a word when designed and set larger than the surrounding text. It is used to introduce a new idea, paragraph, or chapter. We may recognize such elements from books of our childhood, from sacred and historic texts, and from beautiful early editions of classic literature. Whether they appear in illuminated fifteenth-century manuscripts set by scribes or digitally displayed on Jessica Hische's own *Daily Drop Cap* blog, a drop cap letter impresses upon the reader the arrival of something of which to take note, something unique and special that deserves to be savored.

For the book lover, the series is a nod to the tradition of printing and the distribution of ideas, stories, and opinions—ranging from paper to digital media. For the writer and artist, the series pays homage to the significance of composition, texture, and form. With Penguin Drop Caps, we are inspired by the timeless tradition and craft of letters and their endless capacity to communicate.

—E.R.

A young Brahmin named Siddhartha searches for ultimate reality after meeting with the Buddha. His quest takes him from a life of decadence to asceticism, from the illusory joys of sensual love with a beautiful courtesan, and of wealth and fame, to the painful struggles with his son and the ultimate wisdom of renunciation. Integrating Eastern and Western spiritual traditions with psychoanalysis and philosophy, and written with a deep and moving empathy for humanity, Hermann Hesse's *Siddhartha* is perhaps the most important and compelling moral allegory the troubled twentieth century ever produced.

PENGUIN BOOKS

SIDDHARTHA

HERMANN HESSE was born in Calw, a small southern German town in the northern Black Forest, in July 1877. He was the son and grandson of a family of strict Pietist missionaries, a heritage that affected him deeply throughout his life. His grandparents had spent decades of their lives on the Malabar coast of India, where his mother also lived and worked. By the time Hesse was born, however, the family had settled in Calw, though he spent part of his early childhood in a dormitory for missionaries' children in Basel, Switzerland, the main seat of their movement, where his father was teaching. Later, back in Germany, he went through another period of institutionalized living in a Protestant boarding school housed in an old monastery not far from his home. His escape from the school at fifteen years of age became the subject of his novel *Beneath the Wheel*. Both experiences fortified his distaste for authority and his celebration of the individual.

In 1895, at age eighteen, Hermann Hesse struck out for himself by taking work in a Basel bookstore. It took him nine more years of writing, however, to establish himself with his first full-length novel, *Peter Camenzind* (1904), followed by *Beneath the Wheel* (1906), *Gertrud* (1910), and *Rosshalde* (1914), as well as a wealth of short fiction, including *Knulp* (1915). He married Maria Bernoulli of a prominent Swiss family and lived with her and their three sons on the shore of Lake Constance in Switzerland.

A significant change in Hesse's life occurred with the outbreak of World War I. He spent the war years in Bern, Switzerland, working with an agency under the auspices of the Red Cross, supplying books and other amenities to German prisoners of war. After the war and a psychological crisis, his marriage shattered, Hesse removed himself to

Montagnola, a small town in Italian-speaking Switzerland. There—in the relative peace of rural surroundings, interrupted only occasionally by forays into the urban centers of Zurich and Basel—he created his best-known work: *Siddhartha* (1922), *Steppenwolf* (1927), *Narcissus and Goldmund* (1930), *Journey to the East* (1932), and *The Glass Bead Game* (1943). Remarried in his later years to Ninon Ausländer, a Jewish immigrant from Romania who inspired and sustained him in the face of his failing eyesight, he lived out his life in the seclusion of Montagnola. He received many important honors, including the Nobel Prize for Literature in 1946, and died in 1962 soon after his eighty-fifth birthday.

JOACHIM NEUGROSCHEL (1938–2011) translated numerous books from French, German, Italian, Russian, and Yiddish. The winner of three PEN translation awards and the French-American Foundation translation prize, he translated Thomas Mann's *Death in Venice*, E. T. A. Hoffmann and Alexandre Dumas's *Nutcracker and Mouse King*, and Leopold von Sacher-Masoch's *Venus in Furs* for Penguin Classics. He also compiled several anthologies, including *Great Tales of Jewish Fantasy and the Occult*, *A Dybbuk and Other Tales of the Supernatural*, and *The Golem: A New Translation of the Classic Play and Selected Short Stories*.

JESSICA HISCHE is a letterer, illustrator, typographer, and Web designer. She currently serves on the Type Directors Club board of directors and has been named a *Forbes* magazine "30 under 30" in art and design as well as an ADC Young Gun and one of *Print* magazine's "New Visual Artists." She has designed for Wes Anderson, *McSweeney's*, Tiffany & Co., Penguin Books, and many others. She resides primarily in San Francisco, occasionally in Brooklyn.

SIDDHARTHA

An Indian Tale

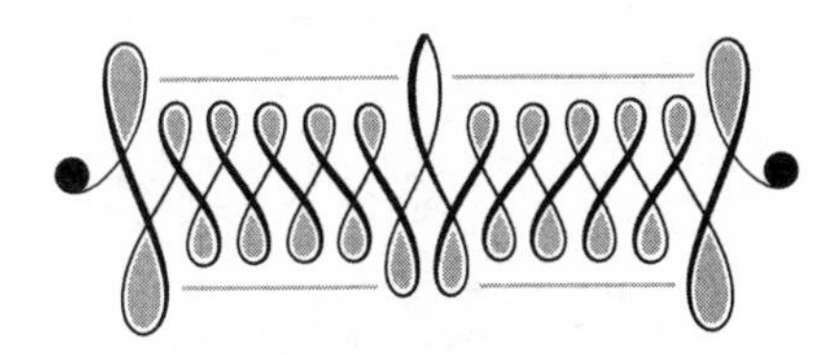

HERMANN
HESSE

Translated from the German by
JOACHIM NEUGROSCHEL

PENGUIN BOOKS

PENGUIN BOOKS
Published by the Penguin Group
Penguin Group (USA) Inc., 375 Hudson Street,
New York, New York 10014, USA

USA | Canada | UK | Ireland | Australia | New Zealand | India | South Africa | China
Penguin Books Ltd, Registered Offices: 80 Strand, London WC2R 0RL, England
For more information about the Penguin Group visit penguin.com

This translation first published in Penguin Books 1999
This hardcover edition published 2013

LIBRARY OF CONGRESS CATALOGING-IN-PUBLICATION DATA
Hesse, Hermann, 1877–1962.
[Siddhartha English]
Siddhartha : an Indian tale / Hermann Hesse ; translated from the German by Joachim Neugroschel.—Hardcover edition.
pages ; cm.
ISBN 978-0-14-312433-7
I. Neugroschel, Joachim, translator. II. Title.
PT2617.E85S513 2013
833'.912—dc23 2013001809

Printed in the United States of America
3 5 7 9 10 8 6 4

Cover design by Jessica Hische and Paul Buckley
Interior design by Sabrina Bowers
Set in LinoLetter Std with Archer

CONTENTS

SIDDHARTHA

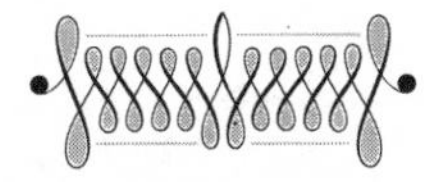

—PART I—

—PART II—

A NOTE ON THE TEXT

Interested readers should turn to the Penguin Classics Deluxe Edition of *Siddhartha* (2003), from which this text is set, for an introduction and suggested further reading by Ralph Freedman.

SIDDHARTHA

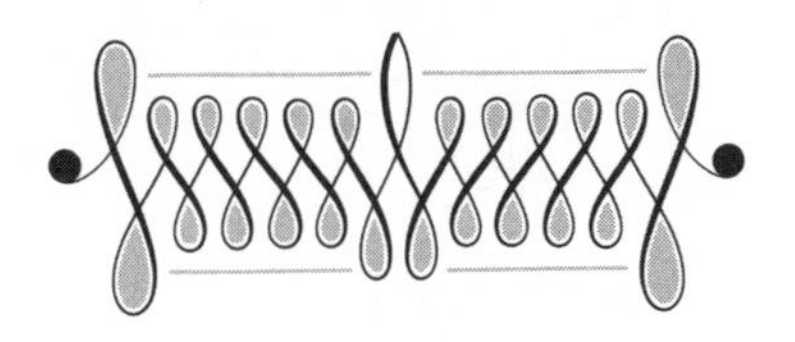

PART I

The Brahmin's Son

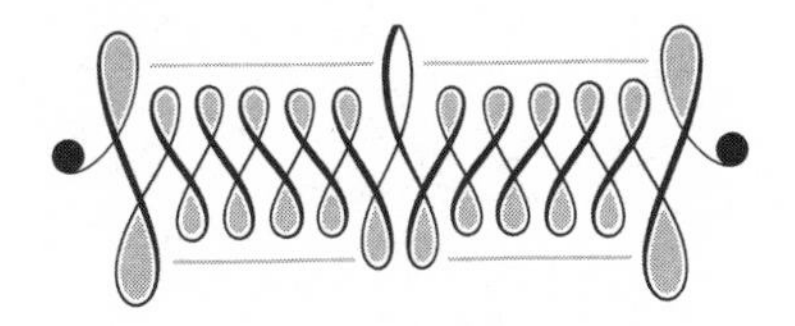

In the shade of the house, in the sunshine near the boats on the riverbank, in the shade of the sal forest, in the shade of the fig tree, Siddhartha grew up—the beautiful son of the Brahmin, the young falcon, together with Govinda, his friend, the son of the Brahmin. Sun tanned Siddhartha's light shoulders on the riverbank when he bathed, when he performed his holy ablutions, his holy offerings. Shade flowed into his black eyes in the mango grove, during boyhood games, during his mother's singing, during the holy offerings, during the teachings of his father, the scholar, during the conversations of the sages. Siddhartha had long been taking part in the conversations of the sages, practicing the verbal battle with

Govinda, practicing the art of contemplation with Govinda, the service of meditation. He already knew how to soundlessly speak the om, the word of words, soundlessly speak it into himself, breathing it in, soundlessly speak it out of himself, breathing it out with all his soul, his forehead enveloped in the luster of his clear-thinking mind. He already understood how to know Atman in his innermost being, indestructible, at one with the universe.

Joy leaped in his father's heart about the son, the intelligent boy, thirsty for knowledge; and he saw him growing up to be a great sage and priest, a prince among the Brahmins.

Bliss leaped in his mother's breast when she saw him, when she saw him striding, saw him sitting down and standing up—Siddhartha, the strong, the beautiful boy, striding on slender legs, greeting her with perfect breeding.

Love stirred in the hearts of the young Brahmin daughters when Siddhartha passed through the streets of the town, with his radiant brow, with his royal eyes, with his narrow hips.

But more than anyone else Govinda loved him, his friend, the Brahmin's son. He loved Siddhartha's eyes and lovely voice, he loved the way he walked and the perfect breeding of his movements, he loved everything that Siddhartha said and did, and most of all he loved his mind, his lofty fiery thoughts, his glowing will, his high calling. Govinda knew that Siddhartha would become no ordinary Brahmin, no lazy sacrificial official, no grasping peddler of spells, no vain and empty orator, no evil, deceitful priest, and no good, stupid sheep in the herd of the many. No—nor did he, Govinda, wish to become any of those, a Brahmin like the other ten thousand. He wanted to follow Siddhartha, the splendid beloved. And someday, when Siddhartha became a god, someday, when he joined the radiant ones, then Govinda would follow him, as his friend, as his companion, as his servant, as his lance bearer, his shadow.

They all loved Siddhartha. He brought joy to all, he delighted them all.

But Siddhartha did not bring joy to himself, he did not delight himself. Walking along the rosy paths of the fig orchard, sitting in the bluish shade of the grove of contemplation, washing his limbs in the daily bath of atonement, sacrificing in the densely shaded mango forest, with perfect breeding of his gestures, loved by all, a joy to all, he nevertheless bore no joy in his heart. Dreams came to him and fretful thoughts flowing from the water of the river, twinkling from the stars of the night, from the sun's melting rays—dreams came to him and restlessness of his soul, smoked from the offerings, breathed from the verses of the Rig-Veda, dripped from the teachings of the old Brahmins.

Siddhartha had started nursing discontent within himself. He had started feeling that his father's love, and his mother's love, and also his friend Govinda's love would not make him happy forever and always, not please him, gratify him, satisfy him. He had begun to sense that his venerable father and his other teachers, that the wise Brahmins had already imparted to him the bulk and the best of their knowledge, that they had already poured their fullness into his waiting vessel, and the vessel was not full, his mind was not contented, his soul was not tranquil, his heart not sated. The ablutions were good, but they were water, they did not wash away sin, they did not slake the thirst of the mind, they did not calm the fright of the heart. Splendid were the offerings and the invokings of the gods—but was that all there was? Did the offerings bring happiness? And what about the gods? Was it really Prajapati who had created the world? Was it not Atman, he, the Only One, the All-One? Were not the gods formations, created like me and you, subject to time, ephemeral? So was it good, was it right, was it a sublime and meaningful act to sacrifice to the gods? To whom else should one sacrifice, to whom else was veneration due but to him, the Only One, Atman? And where was Atman to be found, where did he dwell, where did his eternal heart beat if not in one's own self, in the innermost, in the indestructible essence that every person bore within? But where, where was this self, this innermost, this ultimate? It was not flesh and blood, it was not thinking or consciousness—that was what the wisest teach. But then where, where was it? To pierce there, to the self, to myself, to Atman—was there any other path worth seeking? Ah, but no one showed this path, no one knew it, not his father, not the teachers and sages, not the holy sacrificial chants! They knew everything, the Brahmins and their holy books, they knew everything, they had concerned themselves with everything and with more than everything: the creation of the world, the genesis of speech, of food, of inhaling, of exhaling, the orders of the senses, the deeds of the gods—they knew an infinite amount. But was it worthwhile knowing all this if you did not know the One and Only, the most important, the only important thing?

True, many verses in the holy books, especially in the Upanishads of Sama-Veda, spoke about this innermost and ultimate—glorious verses. "Thy soul is the entire world," they said, and it was written that in sleep, in deep sleep, a human being goes into his innermost and dwells in Atman. Wonderful wisdom was in these verses, all the wisdom of the wisest was gathered here in magical words, as pure as honey gathered by bees. No, there was no disdaining the tremendous amount of knowledge collected and preserved here by countless generations of wise Brahmins.

But where were the Brahmins, where the priests, where the sages or penitents who had succeeded in not only knowing this deepest knowledge but also living it? Where was the initiate who spirited his home in Atman from sleeping to waking, to living, at every step and turn, in word and deed?

Siddhartha knew many venerable Brahmins, above all his father, the pure, the learned, the supremely venerable man. Admirable was his father; still and noble was his bearing, pure was his life, wise were his words, fine and noble thoughts dwelled in his brow. But even he, the man who knew so much: did he live in bliss, was he at peace? Was he not also a seeker, a thirster? Did he not always and always again have to drink, a thirster, from the holy sources, from the sacrifices, from the books, from the dialogues of the Brahmins? Why must he, the irreproachable man, wash away sin every day, strive for purification every day, every day anew? Was Atman not in him, did not the primal source flow in his own heart? One had to find it, the primal source in one's own self, one had to make it one's own! Everything else was seeking, was detour, was confusion.

Those were Siddhartha's thoughts, that was his thirst, that was his suffering.

Often he murmured these words from a Chandogya Upanishad: "Truly, the name of Brahma is Satya—verily, he who knows this enters the celestial world every day." It often seemed close—the celestial world; but he never fully reached it, never slaked his ultimate thirst. And among all the wise and wisest whom he knew and whose instruction he partook of, none of them had fully reached it, the celestial world, none had fully slaked it, the eternal thirst.

"Govinda," Siddhartha spoke to his friend, "Govinda, dear friend, come with me to the banyan tree, let us meditate."

They went to the banyan tree, they sat down, here Siddhartha, twenty paces further Govinda. Sitting down, ready to speak the om, Siddhartha, murmuring, repeated the verses:

Om is bow, the arrow is soul,
Brahma is the arrow's goal,
It must be struck unswervingly.

When the usual span of meditation was ended, Govinda rose to his feet. Evening had come. It was time for the ablutions of the evening hour. He called Siddhartha's name. Siddhartha did not respond. Siddhartha sat absorbed, his eyes rigidly fixed on a very far goal, the tip of his tongue protruding slightly between his teeth; he seemed not to be breathing. Thus he sat, wrapped in meditation, thinking om, his soul sent out as an arrow to Brahma.

Once, samanas had passed through Siddhartha's town, wandering ascetics, three gaunt, spent men, not old, not young, with dusty and bloody shoulders, well-nigh naked, singed by the sun, circled by solitude, foe and foreign to the world, strangers and haggard jackals in the realm of men. From them a hot scent of silent passion came wafting, a scent of devastating service, of pitiless unselfing.

In the evening, after the hour of contemplation, Siddhartha said to Govinda: "Tomorrow morning, my friend, Siddhartha will join the samanas. He will become a samana."

Govinda blanched upon hearing those words, and in his friend's immobile face he read the resolve, as undivertible as the arrow shot from the bow. Instantly and at first glance, Govinda realized: Now it is beginning, now Siddhartha is following his path, now his destiny is starting to sprout, and mine with his. And he turned as pale as a dried banana peel.

"Oh, Siddhartha," he cried, "will your father allow this?"

Siddhartha looked at him as if awakening from sleep. Swift as an arrow he read Govinda's soul, read the fear, read the devotion.

"Oh, Govinda," he murmured, "let us not waste words. Tomorrow at daybreak, I will begin the life of the samanas. Do not speak about it anymore."

Siddhartha entered the room where his father was sitting on a mat of bast. The son stepped behind the father and stood there until his father sensed that someone was standing behind him. The Brahmin spoke: "Is that you, Siddhartha? Then say what you have come to say."

Siddhartha spoke: "With your permission, my father. I have come to say that I long to leave your house tomorrow and join the ascetics. My longing is to become a samana. May my father have nothing against it."

The Brahmin was silent, and silent so long that the stars were wandering across the small window, changing their patterns, by the time the silence in the room ended. Mute and motionless, the son stood with crossed arms; mute and motionless, the father sat on the mat, and the stars drifted across the sky. Then the father said: "It is not fitting for a Brahmin to speak angry and violent words. But indignation moves my heart. I do not wish to hear that request a second time from your lips."

Slowly the Brahmin rose; Siddhartha stood mute with crossed arms.

"What are you waiting for?" asked the father.

Siddhartha said, "You know what."

Indignant, the father left the room; indignant, he sought his bed and lay down.

An hour later, since no sleep came to his eyes, the

Brahmin got up, paced to and fro, stepped out of the house. He peered through the small window into the room; there he saw Siddhartha standing, with crossed arms, unmoved. His light-colored robe shimmered pale. With distress in his heart, the father returned to his bed.

An hour later, since no sleep came to his eyes, the Brahmin got up again, paced to and fro, stepped out of the house, saw the risen moon. He peered through the window into the room: there stood Siddhartha, unmoved, with crossed arms, the moonlight mirrored by his bare shins. With anxiety in his heart, his father went back to his bed.

And he came again an hour later, and came again two hours later, peered through the small window, saw Siddhartha standing, in the moonlight, in the starlight, in the darkness. And came again from hour to hour, silent, peered into the room, saw the unmoved stander, filled his heart with anger, filled his heart with apprehension, filled his heart with fear, filled it with sorrow.

And in the final hour of night, before the day began, he returned, stepped into the room, and saw the youth standing there, and he looked big and foreign.

"Siddhartha," he said, "what are you waiting for?"

"You know what."

"Will you keep standing and waiting until the day becomes noon, becomes evening?"

"I will stand and wait."

"You will grow tired, Siddhartha."

"I will grow tired."

"You will fall asleep, Siddhartha."

"I will not fall asleep."

"You will die, Siddhartha."

"I will die."

"And would you rather die than obey your father?"

"Siddhartha has always obeyed his father."

"Then you will give up your plan?"

"Siddhartha will do what his father will say."

The first gleam of day entered the room. The Brahmin saw that Siddhartha's knees were quivering slightly. He saw no quivering in his face, Siddhartha's eyes gazed far away. Now the father realized that Siddhartha was no longer with him and in his homeland, that he had already left him.

The father touched Siddhartha's shoulder.

"You will," he said, "go into the forest and become a samana. If you find bliss in the forest, then come and teach me bliss. If you find disillusion, then come back, and let us jointly sacrifice to the gods again. Now go and kiss your mother, tell her where you are going. But for me it is time to go to the river and perform the first ablution."

He removed his hand from his son's shoulder and went out.

Siddhartha reeled when he tried to walk. He subdued his limbs, bowed to his father, and went to his mother to do as his father had said.

When, in the first light of day, walking slowly on numb legs, he left the still-silent town, a shadow crouching by the last hut stood up and joined the pilgrim: it was Govinda.

"You have come," said Siddhartha, and smiled.

"I have come," said Govinda.

Among the Samanas

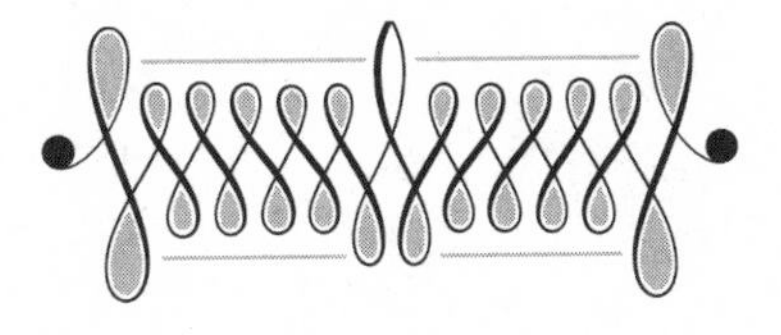

That evening they caught up with the ascetics, the gaunt samanas, and offered them fellowship and obedience. They were accepted.

Siddhartha gave his robe away to a poor Brahmin in the street. All he now wore was the loincloth and the unstitched, earth-colored cloak. He ate only once a day, and no cooked food. He fasted for two weeks. He fasted for four weeks. The flesh vanished from his thighs and cheeks. Hot dreams flared from his enlarged eyes, the nails grew long on his withering fingers, as did, on his chin, the dry and bristly beard. His gaze grew icy when it encountered women; his mouth curled in scorn when he walked through a town with people in lovely clothes. He saw dealers dealing, princes hunting, mourners mourning their dead, whores offering themselves, doctors tending patients, priests setting the day of sowing, lovers loving, mothers nursing their babies—and everything was unworthy of his eyes, everything lied, everything stank, everything stank of lies, everything shammed meaning and happiness and beauty, and everything was unacknowledged decay. The world tasted bitter. Life was torture.

Siddhartha had a goal, a single one: to become empty—empty of thirst, empty of desire, empty of dreams, empty of joy and sorrow. To die away from himself, no longer be self, to find peace with an emptied heart, to be open to miracles in unselfed thinking: that was his goal. When the entire self was transcended and extinct, when every drive and every mania in the heart had fallen silent, then the ultimate was bound to awaken, the innermost essence, which is no longer ego, the great secret.

Siddhartha stood silent in the vertical blaze of the sun, burning with pain, burning with thirst, and he stood till he felt no pain or thirst. He stood silent in the rainy season, the water dripping from his hair, over freezing shoulders, over freezing hips and legs, and the penitent stood until his legs and shoulders were no longer freezing, until they fell silent, until they were still. Silently he crouched in the twisting brambles, the blood dripping from his burning skin, the pus from abscesses, and Siddhartha lingered rigid, lingered motionless until no more blood flowed, until nothing more pricked, until nothing more burned.

Siddhartha sat upright and learned to save breath, learned to get on with little breath, learned to stop breath. Beginning with breath, he learned how to calm his heartbeat, learned how to lessen the strokes until there were few and almost none.

Taught by the eldest of the samanas, Siddhartha practiced unselfing, practiced meditation, according to the samana rules. A heron flew over the bamboo forest—and Siddhartha took the heron into his soul, flew over forests and mountains, was a heron, ate fish, hungered heron hunger, spoke heron croaking, died heron death. A dead jackal lay on the sandy bank, and Siddhartha's soul slipped into the cadaver, was a dead jackal, lay on the shore, swelled, stank, rotted, was shredded by hyenas, was skinned by vultures, became a skeleton, became dust, wafted into the fields. And Siddhartha's soul returned, was dead, was rotted, was dispersed, had tasted the dismal drunkenness of the cycle of life, waited in new thirst like a hunter, waited for the gap through which he could escape the cycle, where the end of causes came, where painless eternity began.

He killed his senses, he killed his memory, he slipped from his ego into a thousand different formations. He was animal, was carcass, was rock, was wood, was water, and he always found himself again upon awakening. Sun was shining or moon, he was self again, swinging in the cycle, felt thirst, overcame thirst, felt new thirst.

Siddhartha learned much among the samanas, he learned to follow many paths away from his ego. He followed the path of unselfing through pain, through the voluntary suffering and overcoming of pain, of hunger, of thirst, of fatigue. He followed the path of unselfing through meditation, through thinking till the mind was empty of all notions. He learned to follow those and other paths, he left his self a thousand times, for hours on end and days on end he lingered in the nonself. But though the paths led away from the ego, in the end they always led back to the ego. Though Siddhartha fled his ego a thousand times, dwelling in nothingness, in animal, in rock, the return was inevitable since he found himself again, in sunlight or in moonlight, in shade or in rain, and again was ego and Siddhartha, and again felt the torment of the onerous cycle.

Next to him lived Govinda, his shadow, following the same paths, undergoing the same efforts. They seldom spoke more to each other than was required by service and exercises. Sometimes the two of them walked through the villages, begging food for themselves and their teachers.

"What do you think, Govinda," Siddhartha once said during their begging, "what do you think? Have we made progress? Have we reached goals?"

Govinda replied: "We have learned, and we are learning more. You will become a great samana, Siddhartha. You have learned every exercise quickly, the old samanas often admire you. Someday you will become a saint, O Siddhartha."

Siddhartha said: "It does not seem that way to me, my friend. What I have learned so far among the samanas, O Govinda, I could have learned more quickly and more simply. I could have learned it in any tavern of a red-light district, my friend, among the draymen and dicers."

Govinda said: "Siddhartha is joking with me. How could you have learned meditation, how could you have learned to hold your breath, how could you have learned insensitivity to pain and hunger there among those miserable people?"

And Siddhartha murmured, as if to himself:

"What is meditation? What is abandonment of the body? What is fasting? What is holding of the breath? It is flight from the ego, it is a brief breakout from the torture of ego, it is a brief numbing of pain and of the senselessness of life. The same flight, the same brief numbing is found by the ox driver at the inn when he drinks a few cups of rice wine or fermented coconut milk. He then no longer feels his self, he then no longer feels the pains of life, he then finds brief numbing. Asleep over his cup of rice wine, he finds what Siddhartha and Govinda find when they slip away from their bodies after long exercises and linger in the nonself. That is the way it is, O Govinda."

Govinda said: "You say that, O friend, and yet you know that Siddhartha is no ox driver and a samana no drunkard. The drinker may find numbing, he may find brief flight and rest, but he returns from his illusion, and finds everything unchanged. He has grown no wiser, has gathered no knowledge, has ascended no levels."

And Siddhartha said with a smile: "I do not know, I have never been a drinker. But in my exercises and meditations, I have found only brief numbing and I am still as far from wisdom, from redemption as when I was a baby in my mother's womb—that I know, O Govinda, that I know."

Another time, when Siddhartha and Govinda left the forest and went to the village, begging food for their brothers and their teacher, Siddhartha again spoke: "Now tell me, Govinda, are we really on the right path? Are we really approaching knowledge? Are we really approaching redemption? Or are we not perhaps going in a circle—we who thought we were escaping the cycle?"

Govinda said: "We have learned a lot, Siddhartha, we still have a lot to learn. We are not going in a circle, we are going upward. The circle is a spiral, we have already ascended several levels."

Siddhartha replied: "How old do you think our eldest samana is, our venerable teacher?"

Govinda said: "Our eldest may be sixty years old."

And Siddhartha: "He has turned sixty and has not reached Nirvana. He will turn seventy and eighty, and you and I, we will get almost as old and we will practice, and we will fast and we will meditate. But we will never reach Nirvana, not he, not we. O Govinda, I believe that of all the samanas, perhaps not one, not one will reach Nirvana. We find consolations, we find numbings, we learn skillful ways to deceive ourselves. But the essential thing, the path of paths—that we do not find."

"Please do not," said Govinda, "speak such terrifying words, Siddhartha! Among so many learned men, among so many Brahmins, among so many strict and venerable samanas, among so many seekers, so many ardent strivers, so many saintly men, how could no one have found the path of paths?"

But Siddhartha said in a voice containing as much sadness as mockery, in a soft, in a somewhat sad and somewhat mocking voice: "Soon, Govinda, your friend will leave this path of the samanas, which he has followed with you for such a long time. I suffer from thirst, O Govinda, and my thirst has not lessened on this long samana path. I have always thirsted for knowledge, I have always been full of questions. I have questioned the Brahmins year after year, and I have questioned the holy Vedas year after year. Perhaps, O Govinda, it would have been just as good, would have been just as smart and just as beneficial to question the rhinoceros bird or the chimpanzee. I have taken a long time and I still have not finished in order to learn, O Govinda, that one can learn nothing! There is, I believe, no such thing as what we call 'learning.' There is, O my friend, only one knowledge: it is everywhere, it is Atman, it is in me and in you and in every being. And I am starting to believe that this knowledge has no worse enemy than the wish to know, than learning."

Now Govinda halted on the path, raised his hands, and said: "Please, Siddhartha, do not terrify your friend with such talk! Your words arouse terror in my heart. And just think: Where would the holiness of prayers be, where would the venerability of the Brahmins be, where the holiness of the samanas, if what you say were true, if there were no such thing as learning?! What, O Siddhartha, what would become of everything that is holy on earth, valuable, venerable?!"

And Govinda murmured verses to himself, verses from an Upanishad:

When the purified and pondering mind is
absorbed in Atman,
The bliss of the heart cannot be stated in words.

But Siddhartha kept silent. He thought about the words that Govinda had spoken to him, and thought the words all the way through.

Yes, he thought, standing with a bowed head: What would be left of everything that seemed holy to us? What is left? What turns out to be true? And he shook his head.

Once, after the two youths had spent some three years with the samanas, sharing their exercises, a report, a rumor, a legend reached them through various roads and roundabout routes: someone had appeared, named Gautama, the Sublime One, the Buddha. He had supposedly overcome the sorrow of the world in himself and had stopped the wheel of rebirths. Teaching and surrounded by disciples, he was wandering through the land, with no property, with no home, with no wife, in the yellow cloak of an ascetic, but with a serene brow: a blissful man. And Brahmins and princes were bowing to him and becoming his followers.

This legend, this rumor, this tale resounded, fragrantly wafted up, here and there: in the towns the Brahmins talked about it, in the forests the samanas. The name of Gautama, the Buddha, kept reaching the ears of the youths, for better or for worse, with praise or with scorn.

When the plague is raging in a country, and there is news of a man, a sage, an expert, whose speech and breath suffice to heal the stricken, and this news crosses the country, and everyone talks about it, many believe, many doubt, but soon many set out to seek the sage, the helper. And this was similar: the legend, the fragrant legend of Gautama, the Buddha, the sage from the caste of the Sakyas, was crisscrossing the land. He possessed, said the believers, supreme knowledge, he remembered his earlier lives, he had reached Nirvana and would never return to the cycle, never submerge in the troubled river of formations. Many splendid and incredible stories were told about him: he had worked miracles, had vanquished the devil, had spoken with the gods. But enemies and nonbelievers said that this Gautama was a vain seducer, who spent his days in luxurious pleasure, scorned sacrifices, lacked learning, and performed neither exercises nor castigations.

The rumors about the Buddha sounded sweet; these reports were redolent with magic. After all, the world was ill, life was hard to endure—and lo, here a source seemed to spring, here a messenger seemed to be calling, a mild and comforting call, full of noble promises. Wherever the rumor about the Buddha rang out, the youths all over India sat up and took notice, felt yearning, felt hope, and among the Brahmin sons in the towns and villages every pilgrim or stranger was welcome if he brought news of him, the Sublime One, the Sakyamuni.

And the rumors reached the samanas in the forest too, and Siddhartha too, and Govinda too, slowly, drop by drop, each drop heavy with hope, each drop heavy with doubt. They barely spoke about it, for the eldest of the samanas was no friend of this legend. He had heard that this alleged Buddha had once been an ascetic and had lived in the forest, but then had turned back to luxury and worldly pleasure. And so the eldest had no esteem for this Gautama.

"O Siddhartha," Govinda once said to his friend, "I was in the village today, and a Brahmin asked me into his house, and in his house there was a Brahmin's son from Magadha, and he had seen the Buddha with his own eyes and had heard him teach. Really, my breath was painful in my chest, and I thought to myself: If only I, if only both of us, if Siddhartha and I, live long enough to hear the Teaching from the lips of that Perfect One! Tell me, friend, should we not also go there and hear the Teaching from the lips of the Buddha?"

Siddhartha said: "O Govinda, I had always thought

Govinda would remain with the samanas, I had always thought it was his goal to turn sixty and seventy and to keep practicing the skills and exercises that are the resources of the samana. But lo, I knew Govinda too little, I knew so little about his heart. So now you, dearest friend, wish to enter a path and go where the Buddha is proclaiming his Teaching."

Govinda said: "You prefer to scoff. Scoff all you like, Siddhartha! But has not a longing, a desire awoken also in you to hear this Teaching? And did you not once say to me that you would not follow the path of the samanas much longer?"

Now Siddhartha laughed in his fashion, his voice tinged with a touch of sadness and a touch of mockery, and he said: "You have spoken well, Govinda, well, and you recall correctly. But please also recall what else you heard me say—namely, that I have become weary and distrustful of teaching and learning, and that I have little faith in words that come to us from teachers. But fine, dear friend, I am ready to hear this Teaching—though in my heart of hearts I believe that we have already tasted the finest fruit of this Teaching."

Govinda said: "Your readiness warms my heart.

But tell me, how can that be possible? How could the Teaching of the Gautama, before we hear it, have already revealed its finest fruit to us?"

Siddhartha said: "Let us enjoy this fruit and wait and see about the rest, O Govinda! However, this fruit, for which we are already indebted to the Gautama, consists in his calling us away from the samanas! As for whether he has something different and better to give us, O friend, let us wait with tranquil hearts."

That same day, Siddhartha informed the eldest of the samanas about his decision to leave him. He informed him with the courtesy and modesty that befit the younger man and disciple. But the samana was furious that the two youths wanted to leave him, and he railed and ranted.

Govinda was alarmed and embarrassed, but Siddhartha lowered his lips to Govinda's ear and whispered, "Now I will show the old man that I have learned something from him."

Standing face-to-face with the samana, he caught the old man's gaze with his own eyes and with all his soul, spellbound him, made him mute, made him will-less, subdued him to his will, ordered him to soundlessly do what he, Siddhartha, demanded. The old man went mute, his eyes glazed over, his will was paralyzed, his arms dangled: he was helpless, overpowered by Siddhartha's enchantment. Siddhartha's thoughts took possession of the samana; he had to do what they commanded. And so the old man bowed several times, made gestures of blessing, stammered a pious wish for a good journey. And the youths thanked him, requiting his bows, requiting his best wishes, making their farewells as they departed.

On their way, Govinda said: "O Siddhartha, you have learned more from the samanas than I realized. It is hard, it is very hard to spellbind an old samana. Truly, had you remained there, you would soon have learned how to walk on water."

"I do not desire to walk on water," said Siddhartha. "Let old samanas content themselves with such tricks."

Gautama

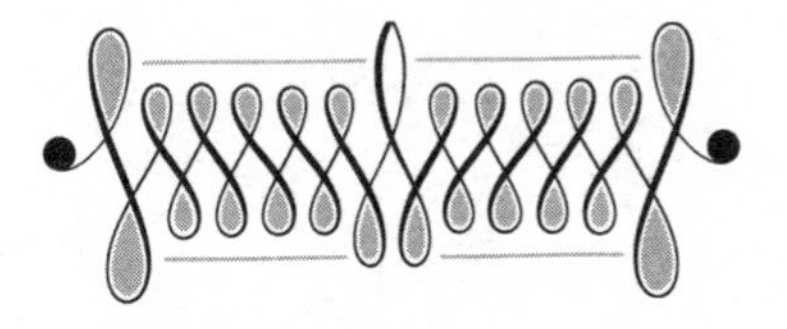

In the town of Savathi every child knew the name of the Sublime Buddha and every home was prepared to fill the alms bowl of Gautama's disciples, the silent supplicants. Near the town lay Gautama's favorite abode: the Jetavana grove, which the wealthy merchant Anathapindika, a devoted admirer of the Sublime One, had given him and his followers.

This area was indicated by the tales and responses heard by the two young ascetics during their quest for Gautama's whereabouts. And when they arrived in Savathi, they were offered food at the very first home where they stopped and begged, and they took the food, and Siddhartha asked the woman who served them the food:

"O benevolent lady, we would like to know the whereabouts of the Buddha, the Most Venerable, for we are two samanas from the forest and we have come to see him, the Perfect One, and to hear the Teaching from his lips."

The woman said: "You have truly come to the right place, you samanas from the forest. You see, the Sublime One is in Jetavana, in Anathapindika's garden. There you pilgrims may spend the night, for it has enough room for the countless people flocking here to hear the Teaching from his lips."

Govinda was delighted, and joyfully he cried: "Fine, then we have reached our goal and our journey is over! But tell us, you mother of the pilgrims, do you know him, the Buddha, have you seen him with your own eyes?"

The woman said: "I have seen him many times, the Sublime One. I have seen him on many days as he silently walked through the streets in a yellow cloak, silently held out his alms bowl at the front doors and carried away his filled bowl."

Govinda listened ecstatically and wanted to ask and hear a lot more. But Siddhartha said they would have to go on. They thanked the woman and left, and they scarcely needed to ask the way, for not a few pilgrims and monks in Gautama's fellowship were heading toward the Jetavana. And when they reached it at night, there were constant arrivals, there were words and calls from people requesting and receiving shelter. The two samanas, accustomed to living in the forest, quickly and soundlessly found a refuge and rested there until morning.

At sunrise they were amazed to see the multitude of the faithful and the curious who had spent the night here. On all paths of the glorious grove, monks in yellow cloaks were walking; they sat here and there under the trees, absorbed in contemplation or in spiritual conversation; the shady gardens looked like a city, filled with people swarming like bees. Most of the monks went into town with alms bowls to gather food for lunch, the only meal of the day. Buddha himself, the Illuminated One, would also go begging in the morning.

Siddhartha saw him, and he instantly recognized him as if a god had pointed him out. He saw him, a simple man in a yellow cowl, the alms bowl in his hand, as he silently walked.

"Look!" Siddhartha murmured to Govinda. "That is the Buddha."

Attentively Govinda peered at the monk in the

yellow cowl: nothing seemed to set him apart from the hundreds of other monks. And yet Govinda soon realized: This is he. And they followed him and contemplated him.

The Buddha went his way, modest and lost in thought. His silent face was neither cheerful nor woeful: he seemed to be smiling inwardly. With a calm, silent, hidden smile not unlike a healthy child's, the Buddha walked, wearing the cloak and setting his feet down like all his monks, according to a precise regulation. But his face and his steps, his silently lowered gaze, his silently hanging arm, and every last finger on his silently hanging hand spoke of peace, spoke of perfection, did not seek, did not imitate, breathed gently in an everlasting calm, in an everlasting light, an inviolable peace.

Thus Gautama walked toward the town to gather alms, and the two samanas recognized him solely by the perfection of his calm, by the silence of his figure, in which no seeking, no wanting, no imitating, no striving were to be recognized, but only light and peace.

"Today we will hear the Teaching from his lips," said Govinda.

Siddhartha did not respond. He was not very curious about the Teaching; he did not believe it could teach him anything new; after all, he, just like Govinda, had heard the contents of the Buddha's Teaching over and over, albeit from secondhand and thirdhand accounts. But he peered attentively at Gautama's head, at his shoulders, at his feet, at his silently hanging hand, and it seemed as if every joint of every finger of this hand contained a Teaching, as if it spoke, breathed, shone, was scented with Truth. This man, this Buddha, was full of Truth down to the gesture of his very last finger. This man was holy. Never had Siddhartha venerated a human being so deeply, never had he loved a human being so deeply as this one.

The two followed the Buddha to town and returned silently to the grove, for they themselves intended to consume no food that day. They saw Gautama come back, saw him taking the meal in the circle of his disciples—what he ate would have sated no bird—and they saw him withdraw into the shade of the mango trees.

That evening, however, when the heat subsided and everyone in the camp grew lively and gathered together, they heard the Buddha teach. They heard his voice, and it too was perfect, was perfectly calm, was full of peace. Gautama taught the Teaching of suffering, the origin of suffering, the path to the elimination of suffering. Calm and clear flowed his quiet speech. Suffering was life, the world was full of suffering, but deliverance from suffering had been found: deliverance was found by taking the path of the Buddha.

In a soft, yet firm voice, the Sublime One spoke, teaching the four principles, teaching the eightfold path; patiently he went the wonted way of teaching, with examples, with repetitions; bright and still, his voice hovered over the listeners like a light, like a starry sky.

When the Buddha—it was already night—finished speaking, several pilgrims stepped forward and asked to be accepted into the fellowship, took refuge with the Teaching. And Gautama accepted them, saying: "You have listened well to the Teaching, it is well proclaimed. Please join us and walk in holiness to put an end to all suffering."

Lo, now Govinda also stepped forward, the shy youth, and said, "I too take refuge with the Sublime One and his Teaching," and asked to be accepted into the fellowship of the disciples, and was accepted.

Promptly thereupon, when the Buddha had retired to his nightly rest, Govinda turned to Siddhartha and eagerly said: "Siddhartha, it is not my place to reproach you. Both of us have heard the Sublime One, both of us have listened to his Teaching. Govinda has heard the Teaching, and he has taken refuge with it. But you, my honored friend—do you not wish to follow the path of deliverance too? Do you wish to hesitate, do you wish to wait?"

Siddhartha, upon hearing Govinda's words, awoke as if from a dream. He gazed and gazed into Govinda's face. Then he murmured in a voice without mockery: "Govinda, my friend, you have taken the step, you have chosen the path. You have always, O Govinda, been my friend, you have always walked a step behind me. I have often wondered: 'Will Govinda ever take a step alone, without me, prompted by his own soul?' Look, now you have become a man and are choosing your own path. May you walk it to its end, O my friend! May you find deliverance!"

Govinda, who had not fully understood, repeated his question impatiently: "Please speak, my dear friend! Tell me—nor can it be otherwise—that you too, my learned friend, will take refuge with the sublime Buddha!"

Siddhartha placed his hand on Govinda's shoulder: "You have not really heard my benediction, O Govinda. Let me repeat it: May you walk this path to its end! May you find deliverance!"

At that instant, Govinda realized that his friend was leaving him, and he began to weep.

"Siddhartha!" he exclaimed, lamenting.

Siddhartha spoke gently to him: "Do not forget, Govinda, that you now belong to the samanas of the Buddha! You have renounced home and parents, renounced background and property, renounced your own will, renounced friendship. That is the will of the Teaching, that is the will of the Sublime One. You have willed it yourself. Tomorrow, O Govinda, I will leave you."

For a long time the friends walked through the woods, for a long time they lay and found no sleep. And Govinda kept urging his friend to tell him why he did not want to take refuge in Gautama's Teaching, tell him what failing he found in this Teaching. But each time, Siddhartha waved him off and said: "Let it be, Govinda! The Sublime One's Teaching is very good; how could I find a failing in it?"

At the crack of dawn, a follower of the Buddha, one of his oldest monks, walked through the garden and called all the neophytes who had found refuge in the

Teaching; he summoned them in order to put their yellow garments on them and to instruct them in the first Teaching and duties of their rank. Govinda tore himself away, embraced the friend of his youth one last time, and joined the procession of the novices.

Siddhartha, however, walked through the grove, lost in thought.

Suddenly he encountered Gautama, the Sublime One, and when he greeted him in awe, and the gaze of the Buddha was so full of goodness and stillness, the youth plucked up his courage and asked the Venerable One for permission to speak to him. Silently the Sublime One nodded his consent.

Siddhartha said: "Yesterday, O Sublime One, I was granted the privilege of hearing your wondrous Teaching. Together with my friend I came from far away to hear the Teaching. And now my friend will remain with your followers, he has taken refuge with you. But I am resuming my pilgrimage."

"As you please," said the Venerable One politely.

"All too bold are my words," Siddhartha went on, "but I would not care to leave the Sublime One without sincerely imparting my thoughts to him. Will the Venerable One lend me his ear for one moment more?"

Silently the Buddha nodded his consent.

Siddhartha said: "There is one thing in your Teaching, O Most Venerable One, that I admire more than anything else. Everything in your Teaching is perfectly clear, is proven. You show the world as a perfect chain, nowhere and never interrupted, as an eternal chain, linking causes and effects. Never has this been seen so clearly, never presented so irrefutably. Truly, the heart of every Brahmin must leap with joy in his body when he, through your Teaching, sees the world as a perfect and coherent whole, unbroken, clear as crystal, independent of chance, independent of gods. Whether the world is good or evil, whether life in it is sorrow or joy, no matter—it may even be unessential. But the unity of the world, the coherent togetherness of all events, the enfolding of everything, big or little, in the same river, in the same law of cause and effect, of becoming and dying: all this shines brightly from your sublime Teaching, O Perfect One. Yet now, according to that selfsame law, this unity and consistency of all things is nevertheless interrupted in one place: something alien, something new is pouring through a small gap into this world of unity, something that was not here before, something that cannot be shown and proved. That gap is your Teaching about the overcoming of the world, about deliverance. And that small gap, that small break shatters and abolishes the whole eternal and unified law of the world. Please forgive me for expressing my objection."

Gautama had listened, silent and motionless. Now, in his kind, in his clear and courteous voice, the Perfect One spoke: "You have heard the Teaching, O Brahmin son, and good for you for pondering it so deeply. You have found a gap in it, a failing. May you continue pondering it. But be warned, you who thirst for knowledge, be warned about the thicket of opinions and the fight over words. Whether beautiful or ugly, wise or foolish, opinions are unimportant, anyone can follow them or reject them. But the Teaching that you have heard from me is not my opinion, and its goal is not to explain the world to people who thirst for knowledge. Its goal is different: its goal is deliverance from suffering. That is what Gautama teaches, and nothing else."

"Please, O Sublime One, do not be angry with me," said the youth. "I have not spoken with you to fight with you or to fight over words. You are truly right:

opinions are unimportant. But may I say one thing more? I have never doubted you for a moment, I have never doubted for a moment that you are the Buddha, that you have attained the goal, the highest, which so many thousands of Brahmins and sons of Brahmins are journeying to reach. You have found the deliverance from death. It came to you from your own seeking, on your own path, through thinking, through meditation, through knowledge, through illumination. It did not come through a teaching! And—this is my thought, O Sublime One—no one is granted deliverance through a teaching! You cannot, O Venerable One, impart to anyone, tell anyone in words and through teachings what happened to you in the hour of your illumination. The Teaching of the illuminated Buddha contains a great deal, it teaches many how to live righteously, avoid evil. But there is one thing that the so clear, so venerable Teaching does not contain: it does not contain the secret of what the Sublime One himself has experienced, he alone among the hundreds of thousands. That is what I thought and realized when I heard the Teaching. That is why I am resuming my wandering—not to seek a different, a better teaching, for I know that there is none; but to leave all teachings and all teachers and to reach my goal alone or die. Yet I will often think back to this day, O Sublime One, and to this hour when my eyes beheld a saint."

The Buddha gazed silently at the ground; silently his inscrutable face radiated in perfect equanimity.

"May your thoughts," said the Venerable One slowly, "not be errors! May you attain the goal! But tell me: have you seen the multitude of my samanas, my many brothers, who have taken refuge in my Teaching? And do you believe, stranger and samana—do you believe that all these people would be better off if they left the Teaching and returned to the life of the world and of desires?"

"Such a thought is remote from me," cried Siddhartha. "May they all remain with the Teaching, may they reach their goal! It is not for me to judge another man's life! I must judge, I must choose, I must spurn purely for myself, for myself alone. We samanas, O Sublime One, are seeking deliverance from the ego. Now if I were one of your disciples, O Venerable One, I fear that my ego would find peace and deliverance only as a figment, as a delusion. I fear that my ego would actually live on and grow big, for I would then have made the Teaching, made my following, made my love for you, made the fellowship of the monks into my ego!"

With a half smile, with an unperturbable brightness and friendliness, Gautama gazed into the stranger's eyes and bade him good-bye with a barely visible gesture.

"You are clever, O samana," said the Venerable One. "You know how to speak cleverly, my friend. Beware of too much cleverness!"

Away walked the Buddha, and his gaze and his half smile were etched forever in Siddhartha's memory.

I have never seen anyone gaze and smile like that, sit and stride like that, he thought. Truly, I wish I could gaze and smile, sit and stride like that, so free, so venerable, so concealed, so open, so childlike and mysterious. Truly, a man gazes and strides like that only if he has reached the innermost core of his ego. Fine, I too will try to pierce to the innermost core of my ego.

I have seen one man, thought Siddhartha, one single man in front of whom I had to cast down my eyes. I will cast down my eyes in front of no one else, no one. No other teaching will entice me since this man's Teaching has not enticed me.

The Buddha has robbed me, thought Siddhartha, he has robbed me, yet he has given me more. He has robbed me of my friend, my friend, who believed in me and who now believes in him—my friend, who was my shadow and is now Gautama's shadow. But he has given me Siddhartha, has given me my self.

Awakening

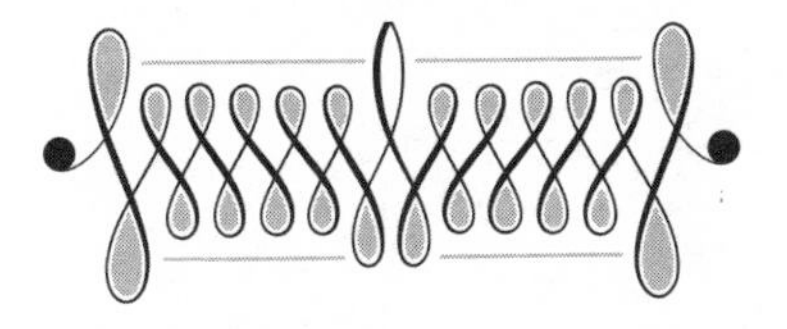

When he left the grove, where the Buddha, the Perfect One, remained, where Govinda remained, Siddhartha felt that his previous life too was remaining behind in this grove and separating from him. This sensation filled him fully, and he mused about it as he slowly walked away. He mused deeply, descending to the very bottom of this sensation as if through deep water, all the way down to where the causes rest. For, it seemed to him, thinking is recognizing causes, and that is the only way in which sensations become insights: they are not lost, they become substance and begin to radiate what is within them.

Slowly walking away, Siddhartha pondered. He

realized he was no longer a youth, he had become a man. He realized that one thing had left him like the old skin that leaves the serpent, that one thing was no longer within him, a thing that had accompanied him throughout his youth and had belonged to him: the wish to have teachers and hear teachings. He had left the last teacher who had appeared on his path, left him too, the highest and wisest teacher, the holiest, the Buddha. He had had to separate from him, had been unable to accept his Teaching.

The ponderer walked more slowly and asked himself: "Just what was it that you wanted to learn from teachings and from teachers and that they, who have taught you a great deal, could not teach you after all?" And he decided: "It was the ego, whose meaning and being I wanted to learn. It was the ego, of which I wanted to rid myself, which I wanted to overcome. But I could not overcome it, I could only deceive it, could only flee from it, only hide from it. Truly, nothing in the world has occupied my thoughts as much as this ego of mine, this enigmatic fact that I live, that I am one and separated and isolated from all others, that I am Siddhartha! And there is nothing in the world I know less about than myself, than Siddhartha!"

The thinking man, walking along slowly, halted, overcome by that thought; and instantly another thought sprang from that one, a new thought: "There is only one reason, a single one, why I know nothing about myself, why Siddhartha has remained so foreign to myself, so unknown. The reason is that I was afraid of myself, I was fleeing myself! I was seeking Atman, I was seeking Brahma. I was willing to dismember my ego and peel it apart in order to find the core of all peels in its unknown innermost essence: to find Atman, Life, the Divine, the Ultimate. But I myself was lost in the process."

Siddhartha opened his eyes and looked around; a smile brightened his face and a deep feeling of awakening from long dreams poured through him down to his toes. And instantly he broke into a run, ran swiftly, like a man who knows what he has to do.

"Oh," he thought, breathing a deep sigh of relief, "I will no longer let Siddhartha slip away! I will no longer start my thinking and my living with Atman and the suffering of the world. I will no longer murder and dismember myself in order to find a secret beyond the rubble. Yoga-Veda will no longer teach me, nor will Atharva-Veda, nor the ascetics, nor any kind of teaching. I will learn from me, from myself, I will be my own pupil: I will get to know myself, the secret that is Siddhartha."

He looked around as if seeing the world for the first time. Beautiful was the world, colorful was the world, bizarre and enigmatic was the world! There was blue, there was yellow, there was green. Sky flowed and river, forest jutted and mountain: everything beautiful, everything enigmatic and magical. And in the midst of it he, Siddhartha, the awakening man, was on the way to himself. For the first time, all this, all this yellow and blue, river and forest, passed into Siddhartha through his eyes, was no longer the magic of Mara, was no longer the veil of Maya, was no longer senseless and random diversity of the world of appearance, despised by the deep-thinking Brahmin, who disdains the diversity, who seeks the unity. Blue was blue, river was river, and even though the One and the Divine lived concealed in the blue and the river in Siddhartha, it was the manner and meaning of the Divine to be yellow here, blue here, sky there, forest there, and Siddhartha here. Meaning and reality were not somewhere beyond things, they were in them, in everything.

"How deaf and dense I was!" thought the swift walker. "If someone reads a manuscript, trying to find its meaning, he does not scorn the signs and letters, calling them deception, happenstance, and worthless peels. Instead, he reads them, he studies and loves them, letter by letter. But I, who wanted to read the book of the world and the book of my own being, I, for the sake of a presumed meaning, scorned the signs and the letters, I called the world of appearances deception, called my eyes and my tongue random and worthless. No, that is past, I have awakened, I am truly awake, and today is the day of my birth."

While thinking these thoughts, Siddhartha halted again, suddenly, as if a serpent were lying in his path.

For suddenly this was clear to him: He, who was truly awakened or newly born, he had to begin his life anew and afresh. That same morning, when he had left the grove of Jetavana, the grove of that Sublime One, when he had already been awakening, already on the path to himself, it had been his intention—an intention that seemed natural and self-evident—to return to his homeland and to his father after the years of his asceticism. But now, only in this moment, when he halted as if a serpent were lying in his path, he also awoke to this insight: "I am no longer who I was, I am no longer an ascetic, I am no longer a priest, I am no longer a Brahmin. What am I to do at home, in my father's house? Study? Sacrifice? Cultivate meditation? All that is gone now; none of that lies on my path now."

Siddhartha stood motionless, and for a moment and for an instant of breathing, his heart froze—he felt it freezing in his chest like a small animal, a bird or a hare, when he saw how alone he was. For years he had been homeless and had not felt it. But now he felt it. Always, even in the most faraway meditation, he had been his father's son, had been a Brahmin, high-ranking, spiritual. Now he was only Siddhartha, the awakened, and nothing more. He took a deep breath and for an instant he froze and shuddered. No one was so alone as he. No noble who did not belong among the nobles, no workman who did not belong among the workmen and found refuge with them, shared their life, spoke their speech. No Brahmin who was not counted among the Brahmins and lived with them, no ascetic who did not find refuge with the samanas. And even the most forlorn hermit in the forest was not all alone: he too was surrounded by ties and bonds, he too belonged to a class that was his home. Govinda had become a monk, and a thousand monks were his brothers, wore his garment, believed his belief, spoke his tongue. But he, Siddhartha—where did he belong? Whose life would he share? Whose tongue would he speak?

From that moment, when the world melted away all around him, when he was alone like a star in the sky, from that moment of coldness and despondence, Siddhartha surfaced, more ego than before, more concentrated. He felt that this had been the final shudder of awakening, the last cramp of birth. And instantly he started walking again, started walking swiftly and impatiently, no longer to his home, no longer to his father, no longer back.

PART II

Kamala

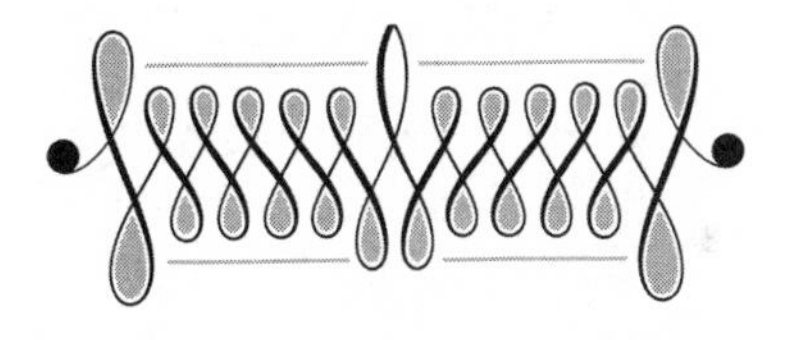

Siddhartha learned something new at every step along his path, for the world was transformed, and his heart was enchanted. He saw the sun rising over the wooded mountains and setting over the distant palm-lined shore. At night he saw the stars arranged in the sky and the crescent moon drifting like a boat in the blue. He saw trees, stars, animals, clouds, rainbows, rocks, herbs, flowers, brooks, and rivers, dew glittering on the morning bushes, high and distant mountains blue and wan, birds sang and bees, wind wafted silvery in the rice paddy. All this, myriad and motley, had existed always; sun and moon had been shining always, rivers rushing and bees humming always. But in earlier times all this had been nothing but a fleeting and deceptive veil in front of Siddhartha's eyes, distrusted, destined to be pierced by thought and destroyed, since it was not reality, since reality lay beyond the visible. But now his liberated eyes remained on this side, he saw and acknowledged visibility, he sought his home in this world, did not seek reality, did not aim at any beyond. Beautiful was the world if you contemplated it like this, with no seeking, so simple, so childlike. Beautiful were moon and stars, beautiful were brook and bank, forest and rock, goat and rose beetle, flower and butterfly. It was beautiful and delightful to go through the world like this, so childlike, so awake, so open to what was near, so without distrust. The sun burned his head differently, the forest shade cooled him differently, brook and cistern tasted differently, as did pumpkin and banana. Short were the days, short the nights, every hour flew by swiftly like a sail across the sea, under the sail a ship full of treasures, full of joys. Siddhartha saw a tribe of apes wandering through the lofty vault of the forest, high in the branches, and he heard a wild and eager singing. Siddhartha saw a ram pursuing a ewe and mounting her. In a reedy lake he saw a pike hunting in its evening hunger, the swarms of frightened young fish darting out of the water, flashing and flickering; strength and passion emanated urgently from the hasty whirlpools created by the ferocious hunter.

All this had always existed, and he had never seen it, he had never been present. Now he was there, he belonged to it. Light and shadow ran through his eyes, star and moon ran through his heart.

On the way Siddhartha also remembered everything he had experienced in the garden of Jetavana, he remembered the Teaching he had heard there, the divine Buddha, the parting with Govinda, the conversation with the Sublime One. He remembered his own words, which he had spoken to the Sublime One, he remembered every word, and he was amazed that he had said things he had not yet really known at the time. What he had said to Gautama—his, the Buddha's, treasure and secret were not the Teaching, but the ineffable and unteachable that he had once experienced in the hour of his illumination—that was precisely what he was now setting out to experience, what he was now starting to experience. He now had to experience on his own. True, he had long known that his self was Atman, of the same eternal essence as Brahma. But he had never really found that self because he had tried to catch it in the net of thought.

The body was certainly not the self, nor was the self the playing of the senses; but neither was thinking the self, nor the mind, nor the acquired wisdom, nor the acquired art of drawing conclusions and spinning new thoughts from earlier ones. No, even this world of thought was of this world, and it led to no goal if one killed the random ego of the senses while fattening the random ego of thinking and learning. Both thoughts and senses were pretty things; beyond them the ultimate meaning was concealed. Both had to be heard, both had to be played with, neither was to be scorned or overrated; and the secret voices of their innermost cores had to be listened to. He wished to strive for nothing but what the voice ordered him to strive for; stay with nothing but what the voice advised him to stay with. Why had Gautama once, in the hour of hours, sat down under the bo tree, where the illumination struck him? He had heard a voice, a voice in his own heart, which ordered him to seek rest under this tree, and he had not preferred castigation, sacrifice, bathing, or praying, eating or drinking, sleeping or dreaming; he had obeyed the voice. Obeying like that, not external orders, but only the voice, to be ready like that—that was good, that was necessary, nothing else was necessary.

During the night, as he slept in the thatched hut of a ferryman by the river, Siddhartha had a dream: Govinda was standing before him, in an ascetic's yellow robe. Govinda looked sad, and sadly he asked: "Why did you leave me?" Siddhartha then hugged Govinda, wound his arms around him, and as he drew him to his breast and kissed him, it was no longer Govinda, it was a woman, and full breasts welled out from the woman's garment, and Siddhartha lay on her breast and drank. The milk from that breast tasted sweet and strong. It tasted of woman and man, of sun and woods, of creature and flower, of every fruit, of every pleasure. Her milk left him drunk and senseless.

When Siddhartha awoke, the pale river was shimmering through the door of the hut, and the dark hooting of an owl sounded deep and melodious in the woods.

At the start of the day, Siddhartha asked his host, the ferryman, to ferry him across the river. The ferryman ferried him on his bamboo raft; the broad expanse of water shimmered rosy in the morning glow.

"This is a beautiful river," said Siddhartha to his escort.

"Yes," said the ferryman, "a very beautiful river. I love it more than anything else. I often listen to it, I often look into its eyes, I have always learned from it. One can learn a lot from a river."

"Thank you, my benefactor," said Siddhartha when setting foot on the opposite bank. "I have no gift as your guest, dear friend, and no fare. I am homeless, a Brahmin's son and a samana."

"I could tell," said the ferryman, "and I expected no fare from you and no gift. You will give me the gift another time."

"Do you believe that?" said Siddhartha cheerfully.

"Certainly. I have learned that too from the river: everything comes again! You too, samana, will come again. Now, farewell! May your friendship be my fee. May you remember me when you sacrifice to the gods."

Smiling, they parted. Smiling, Siddhartha was delighted with the ferryman's friendship and friendliness. "He is like Govinda," he thought, smiling. "All the people I meet on my path are like Govinda. All are thankful, although they themselves have the right to be thanked. All are subservient, all want to be friends, like to obey, think little. People are children."

Around midday he passed through a village. Outside the clay huts, children were tumbling around in the streets, playing with seashells and pumpkin seeds, shrieking and scuffling. But they all shyly fled the foreign samana.

At the end of the village, the path led across a brook, and a young woman was kneeling at the edge of the brook, washing laundry. When Siddhartha greeted her, she raised her head and smiled up at him, and he could see the whites flashing in her eyes. He called a blessing over to her, as is customary among travelers, and he asked how much farther it was to the large town. She stood up and came over to him. Her moist lips were shimmering beautifully in her young face. She bantered with him, asked whether he had already eaten, and whether it was true that samanas slept alone in the forest at night and were not allowed to have women with them. While talking, she placed her left foot on his right foot and gestured as a woman does when she wants to invite a man to have the kind of love pleasure that the handbooks call "climbing the tree." Siddhartha felt his blood warming, and since he recalled his dream at this instant, he bent down slightly toward the woman and kissed the brown tip of her breast. Looking up, he saw her face smiling and full of desire and her narrowed eyes pleading with yearning.

Siddhartha likewise felt yearning and felt the source of sex moving, but since he had never touched a woman, he hesitated for an instant though his hands were ready to reach for her. And at that instant he shuddered upon hearing his innermost voice, and the voice said, "No." All magic left the young woman's smiling face; Siddhartha saw nothing more than the moist gaze of a rutting female animal. He amiably stroked her cheek, turned away from the disappointed woman, and nimbly vanished in the bamboo forest.

That day, he reached a large town before evening and was overjoyed, for he yearned for people. He had lived in the forest on and on, and the night he had spent in the ferryman's thatched hut was the first time in years that he had had a roof over his head.

Outside the town, near a beautiful fenced grove, the wanderer encountered a small train of male and female servants loaded with baskets. In their midst, in an adorned sedan chair carried by four men, sat a woman, the mistress, on red cushions under a colorful sunshade. Siddhartha halted at the entrance to the pleasure grove and watched the procession, saw the servants, the maids, the baskets, saw the sedan, and saw the lady in the sedan. Under high-piled black hair, he saw a very clear, very clever, very delicate face, bright-red lips like a freshly broken fig, eyebrows plucked and painted in wide arches, dark eyes clever and alert, a long, radiant neck rising from a green and gold gown, bright, resting hands long and slender with wide gold bracelets on the wrists.

Siddhartha saw how beautiful she was, and his heart laughed. He bowed deep when the sedan drew near and, straightening up again, he peered into the bright, sweet face, read the clever, high-vaulted eyes for an instant, breathed a fragrance that he was unfamiliar with. Smiling, the beautiful woman nodded for an instant and vanished in the grove, and behind her the servants.

So I come to this town, thought Siddhartha, under a lucky star. He was tempted to enter the grove right away, but he thought the better of it, and only now did he realize how the servants and maids had viewed him at the entrance, how scornful, how distrustful, how chilly they had been.

I am still a samana, he thought, still an ascetic

and beggar. I cannot stay like this, I cannot enter the grove like this. And he laughed.

He stopped the very next person he met, inquired about the grove, and asked for that woman's name, and he learned that this was the grove of Kamala, the renowned courtesan, and that aside from the grove she owned a house in town.

Then Siddhartha entered the town. He now had a goal.

Pursuing his goal, he let himself be slurped up by the town, he drifted with the current of the streets, halted in squares, rested on stone steps on the riverbank. Toward evening he made friends with a barber's assistant whom he saw working in the shade of a shop, whom he found again when entering a temple of Vishnu, and whom he told the stories of Vishnu and Lakshmi. That night he slept near the boats on the river, and early in the morning, before the first customers came into the shop, he had the barber's assistant shave off his beard, trim and comb his hair, and rub fine oils into it. Then he went to bathe in the river.

In the late afternoon, when beautiful Kamala was in her sedan, approaching her grove, Siddhartha stood at the entrance. He bowed and received the courtesan's greeting. He then beckoned to the last servant in the procession and asked him to tell his mistress that a young Brahmin desired to speak with her. After a while, the servant came back, asked the waiting man to follow him, led him silently to a pavilion, where Kamala lay on a couch, and the servant left him alone with her.

"Were you not standing outside yesterday and did you not greet me?" asked Kamala.

"Yes indeed, I saw you yesterday and greeted you."

"But did you not have a beard yesterday, and long hair, and dust in your hair?"

"You observed carefully, you saw everything. You saw Siddhartha, the Brahmin's son, who left his home to become a samana, and who was a samana for three years. But now I have left that path, and I have come to this town, and the first person I encountered before even setting foot in the town was you. I have come to tell you this, O Kamala! You are the first woman to whom Siddhartha has spoken without lowering his eyes. Never again will I lower my eyes when I encounter a beautiful woman."

Kamala smiled and played with her fan of peacock feathers. And asked: "And that is all Siddhartha has come to tell me?"

"To tell you this and to thank you for being so beautiful. And if it does not displease you, Kamala, I would like to ask you to be my friend and teacher, for I know nothing about the art of which you are a mistress."

Now Kamala laughed loudly.

"Never, my friend, has a samana come to me from the forest and wanted to learn from me! Never has a samana with long hair and in an old, tattered loincloth come to me. Many youths come to me, including sons of Brahmins, but they come in beautiful clothes, they come in fine shoes, they have fragrance in their hair and money in their pouches. That, you samana, is what the youths are like who come to me."

Siddhartha said: "I am already starting to learn from you. Yesterday I also learned from you. I have already removed my beard, combed my hair, rubbed oil into my hair. There is little that I still lack, you excellent lady: fine clothes, fine shoes, money in my pouch. Listen, Siddhartha has pursued harder goals than such trifles and has attained them. Why should I not attain what I undertook yesterday: to be your friend and to learn the joys of love from you! You will see that I learn easily, Kamala. I have learned harder things than what you are to teach me. And so: Siddhartha is not satisfactory to you as he is, with oil in his hair, but no clothes, no shoes, no money?"

Laughing, Kamala exclaimed: "No, my worthy friend, he is not satisfactory. He must have clothes, lovely clothes, and shoes, lovely shoes, and lots of money in his pouch, and gifts for Kamala. Now do you know, samana from the forest? Have you noted it?"

"I have noted it well," cried Siddhartha. "How could I not note what comes from such lips?! Your lips are like a freshly broken fig, Kamala. My lips too are red and fresh, they will fit yours, you will see. But tell me, beautiful Kamala, do you not fear the samana from the forest, who has come to learn love?"

"Why should I fear a samana, a foolish samana from the forest, who comes from the jackals and does not yet know what a woman is?"

"Oh, but he is strong, the samana, and he fears nothing. He could force himself upon you, beautiful girl. He could abduct you. He could harm you."

"No, samana, I do not fear that. Has any samana or any Brahmin ever feared that someone might come and grab him and rob him of his learning and his piety and his profundity? No, for they are his own, and he gives of them only what he wishes to give and to whom he wishes to give. It is the same, exactly the same, with Kamala, and with the joys of love. Red and beautiful are Kamala's lips, but try to kiss them against Kamala's will, and you will not get a drop of sweetness from the lips that know how to give so much sweetness! You learn easily, Siddhartha, then learn this too: One can get love by begging, by buying, by receiving it as a gift, by finding it in the street, but one cannot steal it. You have hit on the wrong way. No, it would be too bad if a handsome youth like you were to tackle it so wrongly."

Siddhartha bowed, smiling. "It would be too bad, Kamala, you are so right! It would really be too bad. No. Not a drop of sweetness will be lost for me from your lips or for you from mine! So it is settled. Siddhartha will come back when he has what he is lacking: clothes, shoes, money. But listen, sweet Kamala: can you give me a bit more advice?"

"Advice? Why not? Who would not gladly give advice to a poor, ignorant samana who comes from the jackals in the forest?"

"Dear Kamala, then advise me: where should I go to find those three things as fast as possible?"

"My friend, many people would like to know that. You must do what you have learned and receive money for it and clothes and shoes. There is no other way that a pauper can obtain money. What can you do?"

"I can think. I can wait. I can fast."

"Nothing else?"

"Nothing. Oh yes, I can also write poetry. Will you give me a kiss for a poem?"

"That I will do if I like your poem. How does it go?"

Siddhartha, after mulling for a moment, recited these verses:

Into her shadowy grove came beautiful Kamala,
At the entrance stood the brown samana.
Deeply, upon sighting the lotus blossom,
He bowed. Smiling, Kamala thanked him.
Lovelier, thought the youth, than sacrificing to the gods
Lovelier is sacrificing to beautiful Kamala.

Kamala clapped so loudly that her gold bangles rang out. "Beautiful are your verses, brown samana, and truly I will lose nothing by giving you a kiss for them."

She drew him over with her eyes, he bent his face to hers and put his lips to the lips that were like a freshly broken fig. Kamala gave him a long kiss, and with deep amazement Siddhartha felt that she was teaching him, that she was wise, that she controlled him, rebuffed him, lured him, and that behind this first kiss there was a long, a well-ordered, well-tested series of kisses waiting for him, each different from the next. Breathing deeply he stood there and at that moment he was astonished like a child at the wealth of knowledge and wisdom opening up before his eyes.

"Your verses are very beautiful," cried Kamala. "If I were rich, I would give you gold pieces for them. But it will be hard for you to obtain the money you need with verses. For you will need a lot of money if you want to become Kamala's friend."

"You kiss so wonderfully, Kamala," stammered Siddhartha.

"Yes, I know how. That is why I have no lack of clothes, shoes, bangles, and all beautiful things. But what will become of you? Are thinking, fasting, and writing poetry all you can do?"

"I also know the sacrificial hymns," said Siddhartha, "but I do not want to sing them anymore. I also know spells, but I no longer wish to cast them. I have read the scriptures—"

"Stop," Kamala broke in. "You can read? And write?"

"Of course I can. Lots of people can."

"Most can*not*. *I* cannot. It is very good that you can read and write, very good. And you may also need the spells."

At that instant, a maid came dashing in and whispered something into her mistress's ear.

"I have company," cried Kamala. "Hurry and vanish, Siddhartha. No one must see you here, take note of that! I will see you again tomorrow."

She ordered the maid to give the pious Brahmin a white cloak. Without quite knowing what was happening to him, Siddhartha was dragged away by the maid, taken roundabout to a garden house, given a cloak, led into the bushes, and urgently admonished to vanish immediately without being seen.

Content, he did as he was told. Accustomed to the forest, he slipped soundlessly out of the grove and over the hedge. Content, he returned to the town, carrying the rolled-up cloak under his arm. At an inn where travelers were put up, he stood at the door, silently begged for food, silently received a piece of rice cake. Perhaps by tomorrow, he thought, I will no longer beg for food.

Suddenly pride blazed up in him. No longer was he a samana, no longer was it seemly for him to beg.

He gave the rice cake to a dog and remained without nourishment.

The life they lead in the world here is simple, thought Siddhartha. It has no difficulties. When I was a samana, everything was hard, arduous, and ultimately hopeless. But now everything is easy, as easy as the kissing lesson that Kamala gives me. I need clothes and money, nothing else. Those are small, easy goals, they do not spoil your sleep.

He had long since tracked down Kamala's town house; he went there the next day.

"Things are going well," she cried. "You are expected at the home of Kamaswami, he is the richest merchant in town. If he likes you, he will take you in his service. Be clever, brown samana. I have had others tell him about you. Be friendly to him, he is very powerful. But do not be too modest! I do not want you to become his servant, you are to become his peer. Otherwise I will not be pleased with you. Kamaswami is starting to get old and lazy. If he likes you, he will place a lot of trust in you."

Siddhartha thanked her and laughed, and when she found out that he had eaten nothing yesterday or today, she sent for bread and fruit and regaled him.

"You are lucky," she said as he left. "One door after

another is opening up for you. Why is that? Do you know magic?"

Siddhartha said: "Yesterday I told you that I know how to think, to wait, and to fast, and you felt that these things were useless. But they are very useful, Kamala, you will see. You will see that the foolish samanas in the forest learn a lot of lovely things and can do things that you people cannot do. Two days ago, I was an ill-kempt beggar, yesterday I already kissed Kamala, and soon I will be a merchant and have money and all the things you value."

"Fine," she conceded. "But where would you be without me? What would become of you if Kamala were not helping you?"

"Dear Kamala," said Siddhartha, drawing himself up full-length. "When I walked into your grove, I was taking the first step. It was my resolve to learn love from this most beautiful woman. The instant I made that resolve, I also knew that I would carry it out. I knew that you would help me. I knew it the moment you looked at me by the entrance to the grove."

"But what if I had not wanted to help you?"

"You did want to. Listen, Kamala: If you toss a stone into water, it takes the swiftest way to the bottom. And Siddhartha is like that when he has a goal, makes a resolve. Siddhartha does nothing, he waits, he thinks, he fasts, but he passes through the things of the world like the stone through the water, never acting, never stirring. He is drawn, he lets himself drop. His goal draws him, for he lets nothing into his soul that could go against his goal. That is what Siddhartha learned among the samanas. It is what fools call magic and what they think is worked by demons. Nothing is worked by demons, there are no demons. Anyone can work magic, anyone can reach his goals if he can think, if he can wait, if he can fast."

Kamala heard him out. She loved his voice, she loved the look in his eyes.

"Perhaps," she murmured, "it is as you say, my friend. But perhaps it is also that Siddhartha is a handsome man, that women like the look in his eyes, and this is why good fortune comes to you."

Siddhartha said good-bye with a kiss. "May it be that way, my teacher. May you always like the look in my eye, may good fortune always come to me from you!"

Among the Child People

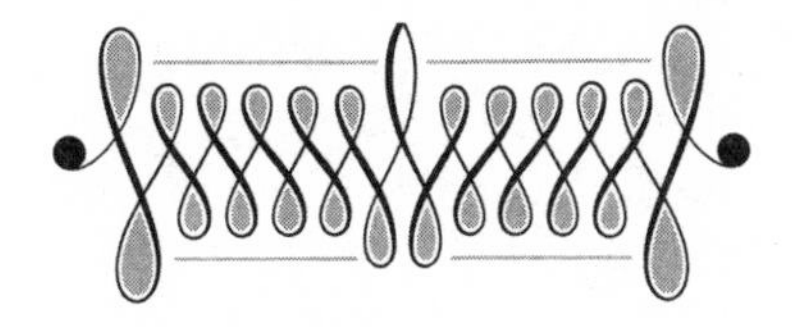

Siddhartha went to the merchant Kamaswami. He was shown into a rich house. Servants led him over costly carpets to a room where he waited for the master of the house.

Kamaswami walked in, a swift and supple man with strongly graying hair, with very clever and cautious eyes, with a covetous mouth. Host and guest exchanged friendly greetings.

"I have been told," the merchant began, "that you are a Brahmin, a scholar, but that you are seeking service with a merchant. Have you fallen on hard times, Brahmin, that you are looking for service?"

"No," said Siddhartha, "I have not fallen on hard

times and have never experienced hard times. You see, I come from the samanas, with whom I have lived for a long time."

"If you come from the samanas, how could you not be experiencing hard times? Are not the samanas completely without property?"

"I own no property," said Siddhartha, "if that is what you mean. True, I possess nothing. But that is voluntary, so I am not experiencing hard times."

"But what do you wish to live on if you have no property?"

"I have never thought about it, sir. I have had no property for over three years and have never thought about what I am to live on."

"Then you have lived from other people's property."

"Presumably. But after all, the merchant also lives off the goods of others."

"Well put. But the merchant does not take from others for free; he gives them wares in exchange."

"That seems to be the way of the world. Everyone takes, everyone gives, that is life."

"But permit me: If you have no property, what can you give?"

"Each person gives what he has. The warrior gives

strength, the merchant gives merchandise, the teacher teaching, the farmer rice, the fisherman fish."

"Very good. And what is it that you have to give? What is it that you have learned how to do?"

"I can think. I can wait. I can fast."

"That is all?"

"I believe it is all!"

"And what use is it? For example, fasting—what good does it do?"

"It is very good, sir. If a person has nothing to eat, then fasting is the wisest thing he can do. If, for instance, Siddhartha had not learned how to fast, he would have to accept any service today, whether with you or someone else, for hunger would force him to do so. But now Siddhartha can calmly wait, he knows no impatience, he knows no plight. He can stave off hunger for a long time and he can laugh at it. That, sir, is what fasting is good for."

"You are right, samana. Wait a moment."

Kamaswami left and came back with a scroll, which he handed to his guest, asking him, "Can you read this?"

Siddhartha peered at the scroll, on which a bill of sale was written, and he started to read the text aloud.

"Excellent," said Kamaswami. "And would you write something on this sheet?"

He handed him the sheet and a pen, and Siddhartha wrote and returned the sheet.

Kamaswami read: "'Writing is good, thinking is better. Cleverness is good, patience is better.'

"You can write marvelously," the merchant lauded him. "We have a lot to talk about. For today, please be my guest and reside in this house."

Siddhartha thanked him and accepted the invitation and now he lived in the merchant's home. Clothes were brought to him, and shoes, and a servant prepared his daily bath. Twice a day a copious meal was served, but Siddhartha ate only once a day, and he ate no meat and drank no wine. Kamaswami told him about his business, he showed him wares and warehouses, showed him accounts. Siddhartha learned a lot of new things, he heard much and said little. And mindful of Kamala's words, he never submitted to the merchant, he forced him to treat Siddhartha as his peer, indeed more than his peer. Kamaswami conducted his business with care and often with passion, but Siddhartha treated it all as a game, whose rules he strove to learn precisely, but whose content did not touch his heart.

Not long after settling in Kamaswami's home, Siddhartha was already taking part in his host's transactions. But every day at the hour that she set, he visited beautiful Kamala: he wore lovely clothes, fine shoes, and soon he also brought her gifts. Her clever red lips taught him a lot. Her tender, supple hand taught him a lot. In regard to love, he was still a boy, and he tended to plunge into pleasure blindly, endlessly, insatiably. So she thoroughly taught him that one cannot take pleasure without giving pleasure, and that every gesture, every caress, every touch, every glance, every last bit of the body has its secret, which brings happiness to the person who knows how to wake it. She taught him that after a celebration of love the lovers should not part without admiring each other, without being conquered or having conquered, so that neither is bleak or glutted or has the bad feeling of having misused or been misused. He spent wonderful hours with the clever and beautiful artist, became her pupil, her lover, her friend. Here, with Kamala, lay the value and purpose of his current life, and not with Kamaswami's business.

The merchant entrusted him with writing important letters and contracts and got into the habit of conferring with him on all important matters. He soon saw that Siddhartha understood little about rice and wool, about shipping and dealing, but that he had a lucky touch, and that Siddhartha surpassed him, the merchant, in calm and serenity, and in the art of listening to others, engaging them deeply.

"This Brahmin," he said to a friend, "is not a real merchant and will never become one, his soul is never passionate about business. But he has the secret of those people to whom success comes on its own, whether because of a lucky star or because of magic, or because of something he learned from the samanas. He always seems to be only playing at business, it never fully becomes part of him, it never dominates him, he never fears failures, he is never bothered by a loss."

The friend advised the merchant: "Give him a third of the profit on business that he conducts for you, but dock him one-third of any loss. That will make him more eager."

Kamaswami followed the advice. But Siddhartha was unruffled. If he made a profit, he was indifferent; if he suffered a loss, he would laugh and say: "Oh, look, this deal has turned out badly!"

He truly seemed indifferent to business. Once he traveled to a village to purchase a large rice crop. But by the time he arrived, the rice had already been sold to another merchant. Nevertheless, Siddhartha spent several days in that village, regaling the farmers, giving their children copper coins, attending a wedding, and he came home from his trip extremely content. Kamaswami rebuked him for not returning immediately, for squandering time and money.

Siddhartha replied: "Stop scolding, dear friend! Scolding has never achieved anything. If there has been a loss, then let me bear the burden. I am very content with this trip. I have met all sorts of people, a Brahmin has become my friend, children have ridden on my lap, farmers have shown me their fields. No one took me for a merchant."

"That is all very nice," Kamaswami cried indignantly, "but I should think you really *are* a merchant! Or did you travel purely for your pleasure?"

"Certainly," laughed Siddhartha, "certainly, I traveled for my pleasure. For what else? I became acquainted with people and places, I enjoyed trust and friendliness, I found friendship. Now, dear friend, if I were Kamaswami, then the instant I saw that my purchase was thwarted, I would have angrily hastened back, and time and money would indeed have been lost. But instead I had good days, I learned things, I experienced joy, I harmed neither myself nor others with anger or haste. And if ever I go there again, perhaps to buy a later harvest or for whatever purpose, friendly people will give me a friendly and cheerful welcome, and I will pat myself on the back for not having shown haste or anger. So let it be, my friend, and do not hurt yourself by scolding! If the day comes when you see that Siddhartha causes you harm, then say the word, and Siddhartha will go his way. But until then, let us be content with each other."

Futile also were the merchant's efforts to convince Siddhartha to eat Kamaswami's bread. Siddhartha ate his own bread, or rather, they both ate the bread of others, the bread of all. Siddhartha never had an ear for Kamaswami's worries, and Kamaswami had a lot of worries. If a transaction was threatened by failure, if a shipment of wares seemed lost, if a debtor appeared unable to pay, Kamaswami could never convince his colleague that it was useful to waste words of grief or anger, to have furrows on his forehead, to sleep badly.

Once, when Kamaswami reproached him, saying that he, Siddhartha, had learned everything from the merchant, Siddhartha replied: "Do not try to get the best of me with such jokes! From you I have learned the price of a basket of fish, the interest that can be charged for a loan. Those are your fields of knowledge. But you did not teach me how to think, dear Kamaswami. You would do better to learn it from me."

And indeed his soul was not with business. Business was good enough to bring him money for Kamala, and it brought in far more than he needed. Otherwise Siddhartha's sympathy and curiosity lay only with the people whose dealings, handicrafts, anxieties, diversions, and follies had once been as far from him and as foreign to him as the moon. But easily as he managed to speak to everyone, live with everyone, learn from everyone, he nevertheless remained aware that something separated him from them, and what separated them was that he had been a samana. He saw the people living in a childlike and animal fashion, which he both loved and despised. He saw them struggling, saw them suffering, saw them turning gray about things that struck him as not worth this price, about money, about petty pleasures, petty honors. He saw them scolding and insulting one another, he saw them lamenting about pains that the samana smiles at, and suffering from deprivations that the samana never feels.

He was open to anything these people brought him. The dealer peddling linen was welcome, the indebted man seeking a loan was welcome, the beggar who spent an hour telling him the story of his poverty was welcome although he was not half as poor as any samana. He treated the rich foreign dealer no differently than the servant who shaved him or the street peddler who cheated him of pennies when selling him bananas. If Kamaswami came to complain about his worries or reproach him in regard to a transaction, Siddhartha listened, curious and cheerful, was amazed at him, tried to understand him, let him be right, as much as seemed crucial—and then Siddhartha turned away from him, to the next person who desired him. And many people came to him, many to trade with him, many to cheat him, many to sound him out, many to arouse his pity, many to hear his advice. He advised, he sympathized, he gave, he let himself be cheated a bit. And this whole game and the passion with which all people played it occupied his mind as much as the gods and Brahma had once occupied it.

At times he heard, deep in his breast, a soft and dying voice that admonished softly, lamented softly, barely audible. Then for an hour he was aware that he was leading a strange life, that he was doing all sorts of things that were merely a game, that he was cheerful, granted, and sometimes felt joy, but that real life was flowing past him and not touching him. Like a juggler juggling his balls, he played with his business, with the people around him, watched them, enjoyed them; but he never participated with his heart, with the wellspring of his being. The wellspring ran somewhere, as if far from him, ran and ran, invisible, having nothing to do with his life. And sometimes he was startled by such thoughts and wished that it could be granted him to participate with passion and with all his heart in the childlike doings of the day, to live really—to act really, to enjoy really, and to live really instead of merely standing on the side as a spectator.

But he always went back to beautiful Kamala, learned the art of love, practiced the cult of pleasure, in which, more than anywhere else, giving and taking become one. He chatted with her, learned from her, gave her advice, got her advice. She understood him better than Govinda had understood him, she was more similar to Siddhartha.

Once he said to her: "You are like me, you are different from most people. You are Kamala, nothing else, and inside you there is a stillness, a sanctuary that you can enter at any time and be at home in, just as I can inside myself. Few people have that, and yet all people could have it."

"Not all people are clever," said Kamala.

"No," said Siddhartha, "that is not the reason. Kamaswami is just as clever as I and yet he has no inner sanctuary. Others have one even though they have the minds of little children. Most people, Kamala, are like a falling leaf, that wafts and drifts through the air, and twists and tumbles to the ground. Others, however, few, are like stars: they have a fixed course, no wind reaches them, they have their law and their course inside them. Among all scholars and samanas, of whom I knew many, one of them was perfect in that respect: I can never forget him. He was Gautama, the Sublime One, the proclaimer of that Teaching. A thousand disciples hear his Teaching every day, follow his rules every hour, but all of them are falling leaves, they have no law and no teaching within them."

Kamala looked at him and smiled: "You are talking about him again," she said, "you have samana thoughts again."

Siddhartha was silent, and they played the game

of love, one of the thirty or forty different games that Kamala knew. Her body was as pliant as a jaguar and as a hunter's bow; the man who learned love from her was an expert in many pleasures, many secrets. She played with Siddhartha for a long time, lured him, rebuffed him, forced him, clasped him, delighted in his mastery, until he was vanquished, and rested, exhausted, at her side.

The hetaera leaned over him, peered and peered into his face, into his weary eyes.

"You are the best lover," she said pensively, "that I have ever known. You are stronger than others, more supple, more willing. You have learned my art well, Siddhartha. Someday, when I am older, I want to have your child. And yet, my dear, you have remained a samana. You do not love me, you love no one. Is that not so?"

"It may be so," said Siddhartha wearily. "I am like you. You do not love either—how else could you practice love as an art? Perhaps people like us cannot love. The child people can; that is their secret."

Samsara

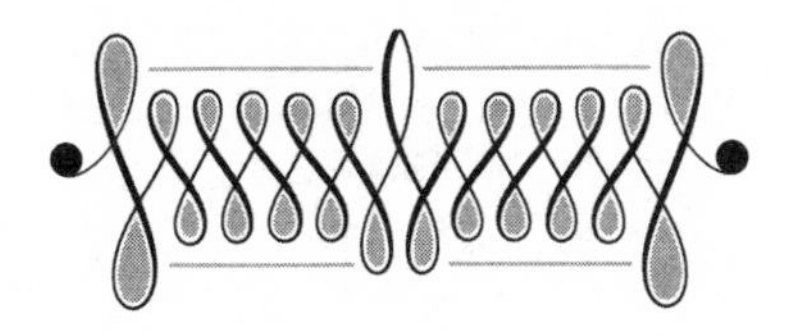

For a long time Siddhartha had lived the life of the world and the pleasures without actually belonging to it. His senses, which he had deadened in his ardent samana years, had reawakened. He had tasted wealth, tasted lust, tasted power. Yet for a long time he had remained a samana at heart; Kamala, the clever woman, had correctly recognized this. It was always the art of thinking, of waiting, of fasting that guided his life; the worldlings, the child people, were still foreign to him as he to them.

The years ran by. Enveloped in well-being, Siddhartha barely sensed their disappearance. He had grown rich, he long since had his own house and his own servants, and a garden on the river, outside the town. People liked him, they came to him when they needed money or advice; but no one was close to him except Kamala.

That high, clear alertness that he had once experienced in the prime of his youth, in the days after Gautama's sermon, after his separation from Govinda, that alert expectation, that proud independence without teachings or teachers, that supple willingness to hear the godly voice in his own heart, had gradually become memories, had been ephemeral. Far and faint murmured the holy wellspring, which had once been near, which had once murmured inside him. Granted, many things that he had learned from the samanas, that he had learned from Gautama, that he had learned from his father, the Brahmin, had lingered in him on and on: moderate living, joy of thinking, hours of meditating, secret knowing of the self, of the eternal ego, which is neither body nor consciousness. Some of these things had lasted in him, but others had gone under and were covered with dust. The potter's wheel, once set in motion, keeps spinning and spinning, and only gradually slackens and comes to a halt; and likewise, in Siddhartha's soul, the wheel of asceticism, the wheel of thinking, the wheel of discrimination had kept turning and turning, was still turning, but was now sluggish and hesitant and on the verge of halting. Slowly, the way moisture creeps into the dying tree stump, slowly filling it and rotting it, worldliness and slothfulness had crept into Siddhartha's soul; slowly they filled his soul, made it heavy, made it weary, lulled it to sleep. By contrast, his senses had come alive; they had learned a lot, experienced a lot.

Siddhartha had learned how to do business, wield power over people, take pleasure with a woman; he had learned how to wear beautiful clothes, command servants, bathe in fragrant water. He had learned how to eat delicately and meticulously prepared dishes, including fish, including meat and fowl, sweets and spices, and to drink wine, which makes you slothful and forgetful. He had learned how to dice and play chess, watch dancing girls, be carried in a sedan, sleep on a soft bed. Yet he still felt different from others and superior to them; he had always watched them with a touch of scoffing, with a touch of scorn, the very scorn that a samana always feels toward people of the world.

When Kamaswami was ailing, when he was angry, when he felt offended, when he was plagued by his merchant worries, Siddhartha had watched him scornfully. Only slowly and imperceptibly, with the passing harvest seasons and rainy seasons, had his scorn grown weary, had his superiority grown stiller. Only slowly, amid his grown riches, had Siddhartha himself taken on something of the ways of the child people, something of their childishness and their anxiety. And yet he envied them, envied them all the more the more he resembled them. He envied them for the one thing that he lacked and that they had: the importance they were able to place on their lives, the passionateness of their joys and fears, the queasy but sweet happiness of being eternally in love. These men were constantly in love with themselves, with women, with their children, with honor or money, with plans or hopes. But this was not what he learned from them, not this, this childlike joy and folly; what he learned from them were the unpleasant things, the things that he himself despised.

It happened more and more often that in the morning, after a convivial evening, he would lie and linger on in bed, feeling stupid and tired. It happened that he became annoyed and impatient when Kamaswami bored him with his worries. It happened that he laughed all too loudly when he lost at dice. His face was still wiser and more spiritual than others, but it seldom laughed and it took on, one after another, those features found so often in the faces of the rich, those features of discontent, sickliness, sulkiness, sluggishness, lovelessness. Slowly he was stricken with the spiritual illness of the rich.

Like a veil, like a thin mist, weariness descended on Siddhartha, slowly, a bit denser each day, a bit dimmer each month, a bit heavier each year. A new garment grows old with time, loses its lovely color with time, gets stains, gets wrinkles, frays out at the hems, and starts showing awkward, threadbare areas. And Siddhartha's new life, begun after his parting from Govinda, had likewise grown old; and so, with the fleeting years, his life lost color and luster, and so stains and wrinkles gathered on him, and, deeply concealed, peeping out here and there and already ugly, disgust and disillusion waited. Siddhartha did not notice. He noticed only that the clear and certain inner voice, which had awoken in him long ago and had always guided him in his luminous times, had now grown still.

The world had captured him: pleasure, lustfulness, sluggishness, and finally the vice that he had always scorned and scoffed at most as the most foolish vice: greed. Property, ownership, and wealth had also finally captured him, were no longer glitter and glamour for him, had become a chain and a charge. It was through a strange and insidious path that Siddhartha had gotten into this final and most despicable dependency: through dice. Siddhartha had smilingly and casually treated gambling as a custom of the child people; but once he had stopped being a samana at heart, he had begun gambling for money and precious objects with mounting rage and passion. He was a feared player, few dared to dice with him—his stakes were too high and too brazen. He gambled out of his heart's distress; losing and squandering the filthy lucre brought him an angry joy: there was no plainer, no more disdainful way to show his contempt for wealth, the idol of the merchants. So he wagered high and ruthlessly, despising himself, deriding himself, raked thousands in, threw thousands away, lost money, lost jewelry, lost a villa, won back, lost again. That fear, that dreadful and oppressive fear that he felt while dicing, while fretting about high stakes—he loved that fear and kept trying to renew it, trying to increase it, to titillate it more and more. For it was only in these sensations that he still felt something like happiness, something like euphoria, something like a heightened life in the midst of his glutted, tepid, insipid existence.

And after every great loss, he schemed to obtain new wealth, more zealously conducted his dealings, more rigorously forced his debtors to pay, for he wanted to keep on gambling, he wanted to keep on squandering, keep on showing his disdain of wealth. Siddhartha lost his composure when losing at dice, he lost his patience with tardy payers, lost his good-naturedness toward beggars, lost his delight in giving or lending money to supplicants. He, who lost ten thousand on a throw of dice and laughed, grew stricter and pettier in business, and sometimes dreamed of money at night! And as often as he awoke from this ugly enchantment, as often as he saw his face older and uglier in the bedroom mirror, as often as shame and disgust overwhelmed him, he kept fleeing—fleeing into a new game of chance, fleeing into a daze of lust, of wine, and from there back to the drive to acquire and accumulate. In this senseless cycle, he ran himself weary, ran himself old, ran himself ill.

Then one night he was warned by a dream. He had spent the evening with Kamala, in her beautiful pleasure garden. They had sat conversing under the trees, and Kamala had spoken pensive words, words concealing sadness and weariness. She had asked him to talk about Gautama and she could not hear enough about him: how pure his eyes, how still and lovely his lips, how kind his smile, how peaceful his gait. Siddhartha had had to talk and talk to her about the sublime Buddha, and Kamala had sighed and had said:

"Someday, perhaps soon, I too will follow this Buddha. I will give him my pleasure garden and will take refuge with his Teaching."

But thereupon she had teased him and gripped him with painful ardor in the game of love, amid bites and tears, as if trying to squeeze the last sweet drop from this vain and ephemeral pleasure. Never had it been so strangely clear to Siddhartha how closely lust is related to death. Next, he had lain at her side, and Kamala's face had been near his, and under her eyes and next to the corners of her mouth he had more clearly than ever before read an anxious handwriting, a writing of fine lines, of quiet furrows, a writing that recalled autumn and old age, just as Siddhartha himself, though only in his forties, had noticed gray hairs here and there in his black hair.

Fatigue was written on Kamala's beautiful face, fatigue caused by going a long way that has no cheerful end, fatigue and the start of fading, and secret, unspoken, and perhaps not even conscious anxiety: fear of old age, fear of autumn, fear of death. He had parted from her with a sigh, his soul full of surfeit and full of secret anxiety.

Then Siddhartha had spent the night in his house with wine and dancing girls, had played the superior to his peers, the superior man that he no longer was. He had drunk a lot of wine and gone to bed long after midnight, weary and yet agitated, on the verge of weeping and despairing, and tried and tried but failed to find sleep. His heart was full of a misery that he thought he could no longer bear, full of a disgust that permeated him like the tepid, repulsive taste of wine, the all-too-sweet and bleak music, the all-too-soft smiles of the dancing girls, the all-too-sweet scent of their hair and breasts.

But above all, he was disgusted at himself, at his fragrant hair, at the smell of wine from his mouth, at the slack fatigue and surfeit of his skin. Like someone who has eaten or drunk too much and vomits it up, tormented, and yet glad about the relief, the sleepless man, in a tremendous surge of disgust, wished he were rid of these pleasures, these habits, this whole senseless life and himself. It was not before the glow of morning and the first bustle outside his town house that he fell asleep, that he found a half numbing, an inkling of sleep for a few moments. And in those moments he had a dream:

Kamala kept a small, rare songbird in a gold cage. He dreamed about this bird. He dreamed that this bird, which normally sang in the morning, had grown mute, and noticing this, he went over to the cage and peered inside. The little bird was dead, lying stiff on the bottom. He took it out, weighed it in his hand for a moment and then threw it away, out into the street—and at that same moment, he was terribly frightened, and his heart ached as if, with this dead bird, he had thrown away all value and all goodness.

Jumping up from this dream, he felt a profound sadness. He had, it seemed to him, been leading a worthless life, worthless and senseless; no living thing, no precious thing, nothing worth keeping had remained in his hands. He stood alone and empty like a castaway on a shore.

Gloomy, Siddhartha went to a pleasure garden belonging to him, locked the gate, sat down under a mango tree, felt death in his heart and horror in his breast, sat and sensed everything withering inside him, dying inside him, coming to an end. Gradually he gathered his thoughts and mentally reviewed the entire path of his life, from the very first days he could recall. When had he ever been happy, felt true bliss? Oh yes, he had experienced it several times. In his boyhood he had tasted it when garnering praise from the Brahmins, when he, far ahead of others his age, had excelled in reciting the sacred verses, debating with the scholars, assisting at a sacrifice. At such times he had felt it in his heart: "Before you lies a path to which you are called, the gods are awaiting you."

And again as a youth, when the goal of all reflection, soaring higher and higher, had torn him out and up from the throng of similar strivers, when he had painfully struggled to grasp the meaning of Brahma, when any attained wisdom merely triggered new thirst in him—at such times, in the midst of thirst, in the midst of pain, he had felt the same thing: "Onward! Onward! You are called!"

He had heard that voice when leaving his homeland and choosing the life of the samana, and again, when going from the samanas to that Perfect One, and then from him into the unknown. How long had he not heard that voice, how long had he not reached any height, how even and bleak his path had been. For many long years, with no high goal, no thirst, no exaltation, he had been content with minor pleasures and yet never satisfied! All these years, unbeknownst to himself, he had striven and yearned to become a human being like these many, like these children; and yet his life had been much poorer and more wretched than their lives, for their goals were not his, their worries not his. This whole world of Kamaswami people had only been a game for him, a dance that one watches, a comedy. Kamala alone had been dear to him, precious to him—but was she still? Did he still need her or she him? Were they not playing a game without end? Was it necessary to live for that? No, it was not necessary! This game was called samsara, a game for children, a game that might be lovely to play once, twice, tenfold—but again and again?

Now Siddhartha knew that the game was done, that he could play it no longer. A shudder ran through his body: inside him, he felt, something had died.

All that day he sat under the mango tree, remembering his father, remembering Govinda, remembering Gautama. Had he left them merely to become a Kamaswami? He was still sitting as night set in. When he looked up and spotted the stars, he thought: "Here I sit under my mango tree in my pleasure garden." He smiled faintly. Was it really necessary, was it right, was it not a foolish game to own a mango tree, to own a garden?

He was done with them too, they died in him too. He rose, said farewell to the mango tree, farewell to the pleasure garden. Since he had not eaten all day, he felt vehement hunger and he recalled his house in town, his chamber and his bed, the table with food. He smiled wearily, shook himself, and said farewell to these things.

That same hour of night Siddhartha left his garden, left the town, and never came back. For a long time, Kamaswami, who thought he had fallen into the hands of highwaymen, sent out men to look for him. But Kamala sent no one to look for him. When she learned that Siddhartha had disappeared, she was not surprised. Had she not always expected it? Was he not a samana, a homeless wanderer, a pilgrim? She had felt this most intensely at their last meeting, and amid the pain of her loss she was glad that she had drawn him so ardently to her heart that last time, that she had felt so thoroughly possessed and permeated by him.

When she heard the first news of Siddhartha's disappearance, she stepped over to the window, where she kept a rare songbird in a gold cage. She opened the door of the cage, took out the bird, and let it fly. She watched and watched it, the flying bird. From that day on she received no more visitors and kept her house locked. After a time she realized that she was pregnant from her last meeting with Siddhartha.

By the River

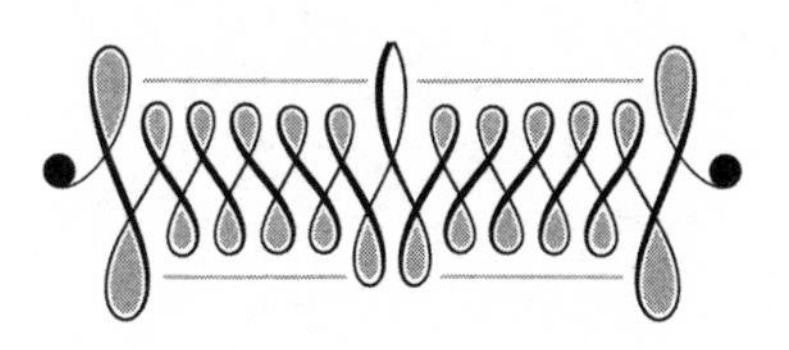

Siddhartha wandered through the forest, far from the town, and knew only one thing: that he could not go back, that this life he had led for many years was over and done with. He had drained it, had drunk it to the dregs, to the point of disgust. Dead was the songbird he had dreamed of. Dead was the bird in his heart. He was deeply entangled in samsara, he had sucked in death and disgust from all sides, the way a sponge sucks in water until it is full. He was full of surfeit, full of misery, full of death; there was nothing left in the world that could lure him, that could delight him, that could comfort him.

He yearned to know nothing more about himself, to find peace, to be dead. If only lightning could come and kill him! If only a tiger could come and devour him! If only there were a wine, a poison that could bring him a stupor, bring him sleep and oblivion and no more awakening! Was there any filth with which he had not soiled himself, any sin or folly he had not committed, any spiritual bleakness with which he had not burdened himself? Was it still possible to go on living? Was it possible to inhale breath again and again and exhale breath, to feel hunger, to eat again, to sleep again, to lie with a woman again? Was this cycle not exhausted and completed for him?

Siddhartha reached the large river in the forest, the same river across which a ferryman had once ferried him when Siddhartha had been a young man coming from Gautama's town. He now halted at this river, stood hesitantly on the bank. Fatigue and hunger had weakened him, and then why should he go on, where to, toward what destination? No, there were no more destinations, there was nothing but his deep, painful yearning to shake off this whole wild dream, to spit out this stale wine, to end this woeful and shameful life.

A bent tree hung over the riverbank, a coconut tree. Siddhartha leaned his shoulder against it, put his arm around the trunk, and gazed down into the green water, which kept flowing and flowing beneath him. Gazing down, he felt entirely filled with the wish to let go and go under in this water. In the water a dreadful emptiness mirrored a fearful emptiness in his soul. Yes, he was at the end. Nothing was left for him but to snuff himself out, but to shatter the failed formation of his life, toss it at the feet of snickering gods. This was the great vomiting he had longed for: death, the shattering of the form he hated! Let the fish eat him, this dog Siddhartha, this madman, this foul and fetid body, this exhausted and misused soul! Let the fish and the crocodiles eat him, let the demons dismember him!

With a twisted face he stared into the water, saw his face reflected, and he spit at it. In deep fatigue, he loosened his arm from the tree trunk and turned slightly in order to plunge in a sheer drop, to go under at last. Closing his eyes, he leaned toward death.

But now, from remote regions of his soul, from past times of his worn-out life, a sound came flashing. It was a word, a syllable, which he lulled unthinkingly to himself, the old initial word and final word of all Brahmin prayers, the sacred "om," which virtually means "the perfect" or "the completion." And the instant the om touched Siddhartha's ears, his slumbering spirit suddenly awoke and it recognized the folly of his action.

Siddhartha was profoundly frightened. So this was the state he was in: he was so lost, so forlorn, so forsaken by all wisdom that he had sought death, that this wish, this childish wish had grown in him, to find peace by snuffing his body! What all the recent torturing, all sobering, all despairing had failed to do was effected by the moment when the om pierced his consciousness: he recognized himself in his misery and his vagary.

"Om!" he uttered to himself. "Om!" And knew about Brahma, knew about the indestructibility of life, knew again about all the godliness he had forgotten.

But that was only for an instant, a flash. Siddhartha sank down at the foot of the coconut tree, laid his head on the root of the tree, and sank into deep sleep.

Deep was his sleep and free of dreams: he had not known such a sleep for a long time. Upon awakening after several hours, he felt as if ten years had passed. He heard the soft flowing of the water, he did not know where he was or who had brought him here, he opened his eyes, he was amazed to see trees and heaven above him, and he recalled where he was and how he had come here. But it took him a long while to remember, and the past seemed veiled, endlessly far, endlessly remote, endlessly indifferent. All he knew was that he had abandoned his bygone life (in the first instant of awareness it seemed like a former, a long-past incarnation, like an early prebirth of his present ego), that he had abandoned his bygone life, that, full of disgust and distress, he had even wanted to throw it away. But he had come to his senses by a river, under a coconut tree, with the sacred word om on his lips, whereupon he had fallen asleep. And now he had awakened and was looking at the world as a new man. Softly he spoke the om to himself, the word on which he had fallen asleep, and his very long sleep seemed to have been nothing but a long and absorbed uttering of "om," a thinking of "om," a sinking and full merging into om, into the nameless, the complete and perfect.

What a wonderful sleep this had been! Never had a sleep refreshed him, renewed him, rejuvenated him so profoundly! Might he really have died, have perished, and been reborn in a new shape? But no, he recognized himself, he recognized his hands and his feet, recognized the place where he was lying, knew this ego in his breast, this Siddhartha, this obstinate man, this bizarre man. And yet this Siddhartha had been transformed all the same, had been renewed, had strangely slept his fill, was strangely awake, cheerful, and curious.

Siddhartha sat up; and now he saw someone sitting across from him: a stranger, a monk in a yellow robe, with a shaved head, and in the posture of reflection. Siddhartha gazed at the man who had no beard, no hair on his head. And after gazing only briefly he recognized this monk: it was Govinda, the friend of his youth, Govinda, who had taken refuge with the sublime Buddha. Govinda had aged, he too, but his face still had the old features, it spoke of zeal, of loyalty, of seeking, of anxiety. But when Govinda, feeling Siddhartha's gaze, opened his eyes and looked at him, Siddhartha saw that Govinda did not recognize him. Govinda was delighted to find him awake; clearly he had been sitting here for a long time, waiting for his awakening although he did not know him.

"I was sleeping," said Siddhartha. "How did you get here?"

"You were sleeping," replied Govinda. "It is not good to sleep in such places, where there are many serpents and the forest animals have their trails. I, sir, am a disciple of the sublime Gautama, the Buddha, the Sakyamuni, and a number of us were pilgriming here: I saw you lying and sleeping in this place, where it is dangerous to sleep. I therefore tried to waken you, sir, and since I saw that your sleep was very deep, I remained behind my brethren and sat with you. And then, so it seems, I fell asleep myself, I, who wanted to watch over your sleep. I did my duty poorly, weariness overwhelmed me. But now that you are awake, let me go, so that I may catch up with my brethren."

"Thank you, samana, for guarding my sleep," said Siddhartha. "You disciples of the Sublime One are friendly. Go now."

"I am going, sir. May you always be well."

"I thank you, samana."

Govinda made the sign of parting and said, "Farewell."

"Farewell, Govinda," said Siddhartha.

The monk halted.

"Excuse me, sir, how do you know my name?"

Siddhartha smiled.

"I know you, O Govinda, from your father's hut and from the Brahmin school, and from the sacrifices, and from our joining the samanas, and from the hour when you took refuge with the Sublime One in the grove of Jetavana."

"You are Siddhartha!" Govinda exclaimed. "Now I recognize you, and I do not understand why I did not recognize you right away. Welcome, Siddhartha, my joy at seeing you again is great."

"I too am joyful to see you again. You have been the sentry of my sleep. Let me thank you again, although I needed no sentry. Where are you going, O friend?"

"I am going nowhere. We monks are always on the move, except in the rainy season. We wander from place to place, live according to the Rule, proclaim the Teaching, receive alms, and wander on. It is always like that. But you, Siddhartha, where are you going?"

Siddhartha said: "It is the same with me, my friend, as with you. I am going nowhere. I am merely on the move. I am pilgriming."

Govinda said: "You say you are pilgriming, and I believe you. But forgive me, O Siddhartha, you do not look like a pilgrim. You wear a rich man's clothes, you wear a nobleman's shoes, and your hair, which smells of fragrant water, is not the hair of a pilgrim, not the hair of a samana."

"True, dear friend, you have observed well, your sharp eye sees everything. But I did not say that I am a samana. I said: I am pilgriming. And that is the way it is: I am pilgriming."

"You are pilgriming," said Govinda. "But few pilgrim in such clothes, few in such shoes, few with such hair. Never have I met such a pilgrim though I have been pilgriming for many years."

"I believe you, my Govinda. But today you have indeed met such a pilgrim, in such shoes, in such garments. Remember, dear friend: Ephemeral, highly ephemeral is the world of formations; ephemeral, highly ephemeral are our clothes and our hairstyles, and our hair and bodies themselves. I wear the clothes of a rich man, you saw that correctly. I wear them for I was a rich man, and I wear my hair like the worldlings and sensualists for I was one of them."

"And now, Siddhartha, what are you now?"

"I do not know, I know it as little as you. I am on the move. I was a rich man, and am no longer one; and I do not know what I will be tomorrow."

"You have lost your wealth?"

"I have lost it, or it has lost me. It has gone astray. The wheel of formations turns swiftly, Govinda. Where is Siddhartha the Brahmin? Where is Siddhartha the samana? Where is Siddhartha the rich man? The ephemeral changes swiftly, Govinda—you know that."

With doubt in his eyes Govinda gazed and gazed at the friend of his youth. Then he bade him farewell as one does with noblemen, and he went his way.

With a smiling face, Siddhartha peered after him; he still loved him, that loyal man, that anxious man. And how could he, in this moment, in this splendid hour after his wonderful sleep, permeated with the om, not love someone and something?! That was the enchantment that had happened to him in his sleep and through the om: he now loved everything and everyone, he was full of cheerful love for anything he saw. And it seemed to him now that he had been so ill earlier because he had been able to love nothing and no one.

With a smiling face, Siddhartha peered after the departing monk. Sleep had greatly strengthened him, but hunger now greatly tormented him, for he had not eaten in two days, and long past was the time when he had been hard toward hunger. With grief, and yet with laughter too, he thought back to that time. He recalled that he had boasted of three things to Kamala; he had been master of three noble and invincible arts: fasting—waiting—thinking. That had been his property, his might and strength, his solid staff. In the zealous, arduous years of his youth he had learned those three arts, and nothing else. And now they had abandoned him; none of them were his anymore: not fasting, not waiting, not thinking. He had given them away for the most wretched things, the most ephemeral things, for sensuality, for luxury, for wealth! His life had indeed been bizarre. And now, so it seemed, he had truly become a child person.

Siddhartha thought about his situation. It was hard for him to think, he basically did not feel like thinking, but he forced himself.

"Well," he thought, "since all these so ephemeral things have slipped away from me again, I am now standing again under the sun, under which I once stood as a little child. I have nothing, I know nothing, I can do nothing, I have learned nothing. How wondrous this is! Now that I am no longer young, now that my hair is already half gray, now that my energy is ebbing—I am starting all over again, like a child!"

Again he had to smile. Yes, strange was his fate! Things were going downhill for him, and now he stood again empty and naked and foolish in the world. Yet he could feel no grief, no, he actually felt like laughing, laughing at himself, laughing at this strange and stupid world.

"Things are going downhill with you!" he said to himself and laughed, and as he said it, he looked at the river, and he saw the river also going downhill, always wandering downhill, and yet singing and remaining cheerful. He liked that, he gave the river a friendly smile. Was this not the river in which he had wanted to drown, once, a century ago, or had he merely dreamed it?

"Peculiar is my life indeed," he thought, "it has taken peculiar detours. As a boy, I dealt only with gods and sacrifices. As a youth I dealt only with asceticism, with thinking and meditating, seeking Brahma, honoring the eternal in Atman. But as a young man, I followed the penitents, lived in the forest, suffered heat and frost, learned how to hunger, taught my body castigation. Prompt and wonderful, in the Teaching of the great Buddha, enlightenment came to me, I felt knowledge about the oneness of the world circulating in me like my own blood. But then I had to get away from Buddha too and from the great knowledge. I went and learned the pleasure of love from Kamala, learned business from Kamaswami, piled up money, wasted money, learned to love my stomach, learned to flatter my senses. I had to spend many years losing my spirit, unlearning how to think, forgetting the oneness.

"Is it not as if I, a man, gradually and very circuitously became a child again, as if I, a thinker, became a child person? And yet this way was very good, and yet the bird in my breast did not die. But what a way it was! I had to go through so much stupidity, so much vice, so much error, so much disgust and disillusion and distress, merely in order to become a child again and begin afresh. But it was right, my heart says yes, my eyes are laughing. I had to experience despair, I had to sink down to the most foolish of all thoughts, to the thought of suicide, in order to experience grace, to hear om again, to sleep properly again and to awaken properly again. I had to become a fool in order to find Atman in me again. I had to sin in order to live again. Where will my way lead me now? This way is foolish, it runs in loops, it may run in a circle. Let it run as it will, I will follow it."

In his breast he felt joy surging wonderfully.

"Where," he asked his heart, "where do you get this merriment? Does it come from that long, fine sleep, that did me so much good? Or from the word 'om' that I uttered? Or was it that I ran away, that my flight is completed, that I am finally free again and standing under the sky like a child? Oh how good is this fleeing, this freedom! How pure and lovely is the air here, how good to breathe! In the place I ran away from, everything smelled of salve, of spice, of wine, of surfeit, of sluggishness. How I hated that world of the wealthy, of gluttons and gamblers! How I hated myself for lingering so long in that terrible world! How I hated myself, robbed myself, poisoned myself, tortured myself, made myself old and evil! No, never again, much as I liked to do it, will I ever imagine that Siddhartha is wise! But this I did well, this I like, this I must praise: that I have ended that self-hatred, that foolish and desolate life! I praise you, Siddhartha: after so many years of folly, you again had an idea, you did something, you heard the bird singing in your breast and you followed it!"

He praised himself, felt joy in himself, listened curiously to his stomach, which was growling with hunger. In these past few times and days he had, he felt, thoroughly savored and spit out a portion of agony, a portion of misery, which he had devoured to the point of despair and of death. Now all was good. He could have remained with Kamaswami for years, acquiring money, squandering money, fattening his belly and letting his soul go thirsty; he could have gone on living for years in that gentle, well-cushioned hell—if this had not come: the moment of utter hopelessness and helplessness, that extreme moment, when he had hung over the rushing water and had been ready to destroy himself. He had felt that despair, that deepest disgust, and he had not succumbed: the bird, the cheerful source and voice in him were still alive; and that was why he felt this joy, why he laughed, why his face beamed under his graying hair.

"It is good," he thought, "to taste everything that one needs to know. As a child I learned that wealth and worldly pleasure are not good. I knew it for a long time, but I experienced it only now. And now I know it, know it not only with my memory, but also with my eyes, with my heart, with my stomach. Good for me that I know it!"

He pondered and pondered his transformation, listened to the bird as it sang for joy. Had this bird not died in him, had he not felt its death? No, something else had died in him, something that had long yearned for death. Was this not what he had wanted to kill in his years of ardent penitence? Was it not his ego, his small, proud, anxious ego with which he had fought for so many years, which had always defeated him, always returned after every killing, outlawing joy, feeling fear? Was it not this which had finally found its death today, here in the forest, on this lovely river? Was it not because of this death that he was now like a child, so full of trust, so without fear, so full of joy?

And now Siddhartha sensed why he as a Brahmin, as a penitent, had vainly fought with his ego. Too much knowledge had hindered him, too many sacred verses, too many sacrificial rules, too much castigation, too much acting and striving! He had been full of pride, always the cleverest, always the most eager, always a step ahead of all others, always the knowledgeable and intellectual one, always the priest or the sage. His ego had hidden away in this priesthood, in this pride, in this intellectuality. There his ego had taken root and had grown, while he thought he had killed it with fasting and penitence. But now he saw it, and saw that the secret voice had been right, that no teacher could ever have redeemed him. That was why he had had to go out into the world, losing himself in pleasure and power, in women and money, had had to become a merchant, a dicer, a drinker, a grasper, until the priest and the samana inside him were dead. That was why he had had to keep enduring those ugly years, enduring the disgust, the emptiness, the meaninglessness of a bleak and lost life, to the end, to bitter despair, until Siddhartha the sensualist, Siddhartha the grasper could die. He had died; a new Siddhartha had awoken from sleep. He too would grow old, he too would have to die someday—Siddhartha was ephemeral, every formation was ephemeral. But today he was young, was a child, the new Siddhartha, and was full of joy.

He thought these thoughts, listened to his stomach with a smile, gratefully heard a humming bee. Cheerfully he peered into the streaming river, never had he liked a body of water as much as this one, never had he heard the voice and metaphor of flowing water as strong and lovely as this one. He felt as if the river had something special to tell him, something that he did not yet know, that was still waiting for him. Siddhartha had wanted to drown in this river, the old, weary, desperate Siddhartha had drowned in it today. But the new Siddhartha felt a deep love for this streaming water and he resolved not to leave it again so soon.

The Ferryman

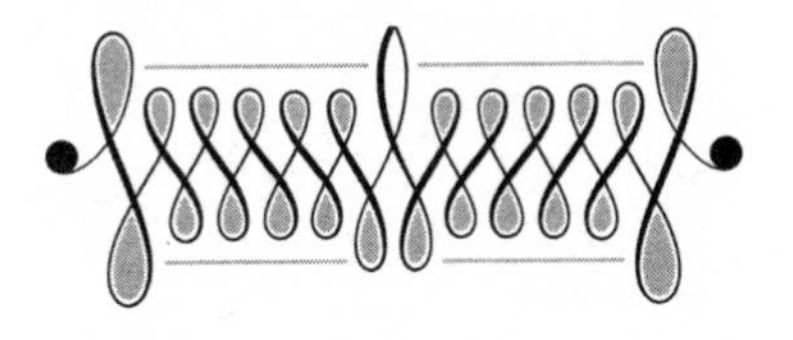

I want to remain by this river, thought Siddhartha, it is the same one that I crossed while going to the child people. A friendly ferryman ferried me then, I will go to him. From his hut my way once led me to a new life, which has now grown old and died—may my new way, my new life start out from there!

Tenderly he gazed at the streaming water, at the transparent green, at the crystalline lines of its mysterious pattern. He saw bright beads rising from the depths, silent bubbles drifting on the surface, sky blue reflected there. The river gazed at him with a thousand eyes, with green, with white, with crystalline, with sky blue eyes. How he loved the water, how it delighted him, how grateful he was to it! In his heart he heard the voice speaking, the newly awakened voice, and it said to him: "Love this water! Stay with it! Learn from it!"

Oh, yes, he wanted to learn from it, he wanted to listen to it. The man who grasped this water and its secrets, so it seemed, would also grasp a lot of other things, many secrets, all secrets.

But of the secrets of the river, he saw only one today: it seized his soul. He saw the water running and running, constantly running, and yet it was always there, was always and forever the same, and yet new every instant! Who could grasp this, who could fathom this?! He did not grasp or fathom it, he felt only an inkling stirring, a distant memory, godly voices.

Siddhartha stood up; unbearable was the roiling of the hunger in his body. Suffering, he wandered farther, along the bank, upstream, listened to the current, listened to the growling hunger in his body.

When he reached the ferry, the boat was ready, and the same ferryman who had once ferried the young samana across the river was standing in the boat. Siddhartha recognized him; he too had aged greatly.

"Will you ferry me across?" he asked.

The ferryman, astonished at seeing such a noble person wandering alone and on foot, took him into the boat and pushed off.

"You have chosen a lovely life," said the passenger. "It must be lovely to live by this water every day and to travel upon it."

Smiling, the rower rocked: "It is lovely, sir. It is as you say. But is not every life, is not every work lovely?"

"That may be. But I envy you for yours."

"Ah, you might soon stop enjoying it. It is nothing for people in fine clothes."

Siddhartha laughed. "I have already been eyed once today because of my clothes, eyed with distrust. Ferryman, would you not like to accept these clothes, which are a burden to me? For you must know: I have no money to pay you the fare."

"You are joking, sir," the ferryman laughed.

"I am not joking, my friend. Listen, you once ferried me across this water for charity's sake. So do it again today, and take my clothes as your fare."

"And do you wish to travel on without clothes, sir?"

"Ah, I would rather not travel farther at all. I would rather you gave me an old apron, ferryman, and kept me on as your assistant or, more precisely, as your apprentice, for first I must learn how to handle the boat."

For a long time the ferryman gazed at the stranger, seeking.

"Now I recognize you," he finally said. "You once slept in my hut. That was long ago. It must have been more than twenty years ago, and I ferried you across the river, and we said good-bye as good friends. Were you not a samana? I no longer remember your name."

"My name is Siddhartha, and I was a samana when you last saw me."

"Then welcome, Siddhartha. My name is Vasudeva. You will, I hope, be my guest again today and sleep in my hut and tell me where you come from and why your lovely clothes are such a burden to you."

They had reached the middle of the river, and Vasudeva rowed harder to buck the current. He labored calmly, with powerful arms, his eyes on the tip of the boat. Siddhartha sat and watched him, and remembered that once, on that last day of his samana period, love for this man had stirred in his heart. Gratefully he accepted Vasudeva's invitation. When they moored on the bank, he helped him bind the boat to the posts. Then the ferryman asked him into his hut, offered him bread and water, and Siddhartha ate with gusto and also ate with gusto from the mangoes that Vasudeva offered him.

Then, as the sun was about to go down, they settled at a tree trunk on the bank, and Siddhartha told the ferryman about his background, about his life, and how today, in that hour of despair, he had seen it pass before his eyes. He talked until deep into the night.

Vasudeva listened very attentively. Listening, he absorbed everything, origin and childhood, all the learning, all the seeking, all joy, all woe. One of the ferryman's greatest virtues was that he knew how to listen like few other people. Without a word from Vasudeva, the speaker felt that the ferryman took in his words, silent, open, waiting, missing none, impatient for none, neither praising nor blaming, but only listening. Siddhartha felt what happiness it is to unburden himself to such a listener, to sink his own life into this listener's heart, his own seeking, his own suffering.

But toward the end of Siddhartha's story, when he spoke about the tree by the river and about his deep despair, about the sacred om, and of how after his long slumber he had felt such deep love for the river, the ferryman listened twice as hard, utterly and thoroughly devoted, with eyes closed.

When Siddhartha fell silent, there was a long stillness. And then Vasudeva said: "It is as I thought. The river spoke to you. It is your friend too, it speaks to you too. That is good, that is very good. Stay with me, Siddhartha, my friend. I once had a wife, her pallet was next to mine, but she died long ago, I have long lived alone. Live with me now, there is room and food for both of us."

"I thank you," said Siddhartha, "I thank you and accept. And I also thank you, Vasudeva, for listening to me so well! Rare are the people who know how to listen, and I have never met anyone who knew it so well as you. This too I will learn from you."

"You will learn it," said Vasudeva, "but not from me. It was the river that taught me how to listen; you too will learn how from the river. The river knows everything, one can learn everything from it. Look, you too have already learned from the river that it is good to strive downward, to sink, to seek the depth. The rich and noble Siddhartha is becoming an oarsman, the learned Brahmin Siddhartha is becoming a ferryman. This too was told to you by the river. You will learn the other thing from the river too."

Siddhartha said, after a long pause: "What other thing, Vasudeva?"

Vasudeva stood up. "It is late," he said, "let us go to bed. I cannot tell you what the 'other' thing is, my friend. You will learn it, perhaps you know it already. Look, I am no scholar, I do not know how to speak, nor do I understand how to think. I know only how to listen and to be pious; that is all I have ever learned. If I could talk and teach, I might be a sage, but I am only a ferryman, and my task is to ferry people across this river. I have ferried many across, thousands, and for all of them my river has been nothing but a hindrance in their travels. They traveled for money and business, to weddings and on pilgrimages, and the river was in their way, and the ferryman was there to get them swiftly across that hindrance. But for a few among the thousands, a very few, four or five, the river was no hindrance. They heard its voice, they listened to it, and the river became sacred for them, as it is for me. Let us now retire for the night, Siddhartha."

Siddhartha remained with the ferryman and learned how to handle the boat, and when there was no ferrying to do, he worked with Vasudeva in the rice paddy, gathered wood, picked the fruit of the pisang trees. He learned how to make an oar, and learned how to repair the boat, and weave baskets, and was cheerful about everything he learned, and the days and months ran swiftly by. But more than Vasudeva could teach him, the river taught him. He learned incessantly from the river. Above all, it taught him how to listen, to listen with a silent heart, with a waiting, open soul, without passion, without desire, without judgment, without opinion.

He lived amiably next to Vasudeva, and at times they exchanged words, few and long-pondered words. Vasudeva was no friend of words; Siddhartha could seldom get him to speak.

"Did the river," he once asked, "also teach you this secret: that time does not exist?"

Vasudeva's face lit up with a bright smile.

"Yes, Siddhartha," he said. "Is this what you mean: that the river is everywhere at once, at its source and at its mouth, at the waterfall, at the ferry, at the rapids, in the sea, in the mountains, everywhere at once, and only the present exists for it, and not the shadow of the future?"

"That is it," said Siddhartha. "And when I learned that, I looked at my life, and it was also a river, and the boy Siddhartha was separated from the adult Siddhartha and from the old man Siddhartha only by shadow, not by substance. Nor were Siddhartha's earlier births the past, and his death and his return to Brahma are no future. Nothing was, nothing will be; everything is, everything has being and is present."

Siddhartha spoke ecstatically; this illumination had made him deeply blissful. Oh, were not all sufferings time? Were not all fear and self-torment time, were not all difficulty, all hostility in the world over and overcome as soon as time was overcome, as soon as time could be thought away? He had spoken ecstatically. Vasudeva smiled and beamed at him and nodded in confirmation, he nodded silently, ran his hand over Siddhartha's shoulder and went back to his work.

And once again, when the river swelled in the rainy season and was roaring mightily, Siddhartha said: "Is it not true, O friend, that the river has many voices, very many voices. Does it not have the voice of a king, and of a warrior, and of a bull, and of a night bird, and of a woman giving birth, and of a sighing man, and a thousand other voices?"

"It is so," nodded Vasudeva, "the voices of all creatures are in its voice."

"And do you know," Siddhartha went on, "what

word it speaks when you succeed in hearing all its ten thousand voices at once?"

Vasudeva laughed happily, he leaned over to Siddhartha and spoke the sacred om into his ear. And that was indeed what Siddhartha had heard.

And little by little, his smile grew more similar to the ferryman's, became almost as radiant, almost as blissful, likewise shining from a thousand tiny creases, likewise a youngster's, likewise an oldster's. Many travelers who saw the two ferrymen thought they were brothers. On many evenings, they sat together at the tree trunk by the bank, silently listening to the water, which was no water for them, but the voice of life, the voice of Being, the voice of eternal Becoming. And there were moments when both, while hearing the river, thought of the same things, of a conversation from two days ago, of one of their passengers whose face and fate occupied their minds, of death, of their childhoods, and both of them in the same moment, when the river had said something good to them, looked at each other, both thinking the exact same thoughts, both blissful at this same answer to the same question.

Something emanated from the ferry and from the two ferrymen, something that some of the travelers sensed. Sometimes a traveler, after peering into the face of one ferryman, began to tell his life story, his suffering, confessed evil, requested comfort and advice. Sometimes a traveler asked for permission to spend an evening with them in order to listen to the river. And sometimes, curious people would come, having been told that two sages or wizards or saints lived by this ferry. The curious asked many questions, but they received no answers, and they found neither wizards nor sages, they found only two old, friendly manikins, who seemed to be mute and somewhat strange and stupid. And the curious laughed and conversed about how foolishly and gullibly the populace spread such empty rumors.

The years flowed away, and no one counted them. Then one day, some monks came pilgriming, followers of Gautama, the Buddha, and they asked to be ferried across the river. And from them the ferrymen learned that they were hurrying back to their great teacher, for the news was spreading that the Sublime One was mortally ill and would soon die his final human death in order to pass into redemption. Not long after that a new group of monks came pilgriming, and then another group, and both the monks and most of the other travelers and wanderers spoke of nothing but Gautama and his coming death. And just as people stream from everywhere and every place to a military expedition or to a royal coronation and gather in groups like ants, so too they streamed, as if drawn by magic, to where the great Buddha was awaiting his death, where the dreadful event was to occur and the great Perfect Man of an aeon was to pass into glory.

During this period, Siddhartha thought a great deal about the dying sage, the great teacher, whose voice had admonished nations and awoken hundreds of thousands of people, whose voice he too had once heard, whose sacred face he too had once viewed with reverence. He thought about him lovingly, saw his path of perfection before his eyes, and smiled as he recalled the words that he, the young Siddhartha, had once addressed to him, the Sublime One. His words, it struck him, had been proud and precocious; he smiled as he recalled them. He knew long since that he was no longer separated from Gautama, whose Teaching he had been unable to accept. No, a true seeker could accept no teaching if he truly wished to find. But the man who had found could approve of every single teaching, every way, every goal; nothing separated him any longer from all the thousand others who lived in the eternal, who breathed the divine.

On one of these days, when so many were pilgriming to the dying Buddha, Kamala also pilgrimed to him, she, once the most beautiful of courtesans. She had long since withdrawn from her earlier life, had given her garden to Gautama's monks, had taken refuge in the Teaching, was one of the female friends and benefactresses of the pilgrims. Upon hearing the news of Gautama's coming death, she, together with the boy Siddhartha, her son, had set out on foot, in simple clothes. She was traveling along the river with her little son. But the boy soon grew tired, he wanted to go home, he wanted to rest, wanted to eat, grew sulky and whiny. Kamala had to rest with him often, he was used to getting his way with her, she had to feed him, had to comfort him, had to scold him. He did not understand why he and his mother had to go on this arduous and dismal pilgrimage to an unknown place, to a stranger who was holy and was dying. Let him die—how did it concern the boy?

The pilgrims were not far from Vasudeva's ferry when little Siddhartha once again made his mother rest. She too, Kamala, was tired, and while the boy chewed on a banana, she squatted on the ground, closed her eyes a bit, and rested. But suddenly she uttered a lamenting shriek. The boy looked at her shocked and saw that her face was pale with horror, and from under her dress slipped a black snake that had bitten Kamala.

They both now hurried in order to find people, and they approached the ferry. There, Kamala collapsed, unable to go on. The boy let out a pitiful cry, while kissing and hugging his mother. And she too joined in his loud cries for help, until the sounds reached Vasudeva's ears as he stood by the ferry. Quickly he came, took the woman in his arms, carried her to the boat; the boy ran along, and soon they all came to the hut, where Siddhartha stood at the hearth, lighting a fire. He looked up and saw first the boy's face, which strangely stirred his memory, recalled forgotten things. Then he saw Kamala, whom he instantly recognized though she lay unconscious in the ferryman's arms, and now he knew that this was his own son whose face had stirred such deep memories, and Siddhartha's heart beat in his breast.

Kamala's wound was washed, but was already black, and her body was swollen. A healing potion was served to her. She awoke, she lay on Siddhartha's pallet in the hut; and Siddhartha, who once had loved her so, now stood leaning over her. It seemed to her like a dream, she smiled as she looked into the face of her friend; only slowly did she realize where she was, remember the bite. She then called anxiously for the boy.

"He is here, do not worry," said Siddhartha.

Kamala looked into his eyes. She spoke with a heavy tongue paralyzed by the poison. "You have grown old, my dear," she said, "you have grown gray. But you resemble the young samana who once came into my garden without clothes and with dusty feet. You resemble him far more than you did when you left me and Kamaswami. Your eyes resemble his, Siddhartha. Ah, I too have grown old, old—did you recognize me all the same?"

Siddhartha smiled: "I recognized you immediately, Kamala, my dear."

Kamala nodded toward her boy and said, "Did you recognize him too? He is your son."

Her eyes grew confused and they closed. The boy wept. Siddhartha took him on his lap, let him weep, caressed his hair, and as he looked at the boy's face, he thought of a Brahmin prayer he had once learned when he himself had been a little boy. Slowly, in a singsong voice, he began to recite it: from his past and his childhood the words came flowing to him. And under his singsong, the boy grew calm, sobbed a little now and then, and fell asleep. Siddhartha put him on Vasudeva's pallet. Vasudeva stood at the hearth, cooking rice. Siddhartha glanced at him, and Vasudeva smiled back.

"She is dying," said Siddhartha softly.

Vasudeva nodded; the fiery glow from the hearth ran over his friendly face.

Once again Kamala awoke. Pain twisted her face; Siddhartha's eyes read the suffering on her lips, on her pale cheeks. He read it silently, attentive, waiting, absorbed in her suffering. Kamala felt it; her gaze sought his eyes.

Looking at him, she said: "Now I see that your eyes have also changed. They are quite different now. So by what do I still recognize you as Siddhartha? You are Siddhartha and are not."

Siddhartha said nothing; his eyes gazed silently into hers.

"You have attained it?" she asked. "You have found peace?"

He smiled and placed his hand on hers.

"I see it," she said, "I see it. I too will find peace."

"You have found it," whispered Siddhartha.

Kamala gazed steadily into his eyes. She recalled wanting to go on a pilgrimage to Gautama, to see the face of the Perfect Man, to breathe his peace. And now instead she had found Siddhartha, and that was good, it was just as good as if she had seen the other. She wanted to tell him, but her tongue no longer obeyed her will. Silently she looked at him, and he saw the light fading in her eyes. When the final pain filled her eyes and broke, when the final shudder ran through her limbs, his finger closed her lids.

He sat and sat, gazing at her lifeless face. He gazed and gazed at her lips, her old, tired, pinched lips, and he remembered that once, in the springtime of his life, he had likened those lips to a freshly broken fig. He sat and sat, studying the pale face, the weary creases, he filled up with the sight, saw his own face lying like that, just as white, just as faded, and also saw his face and hers young, with red lips, with burning eyes; and the feeling of the present and simultaneity permeated him fully, the feeling of eternity. In this hour he felt deeply, more deeply than ever, the indestructibility of every life, the eternity of every instant.

When he rose, Vasudeva had prepared rice for him. But Siddhartha did not eat. In the stable, where their goat was, the two old men arranged a litter, and Vasudeva went to bed. But Siddhartha went out and sat in front of the hut all night, listening to the river, awash with the past, touched and enfolded by all the times of his life at once. Sometimes he stood up, walked to the door of the hut, and listened to see if the boy was asleep.

Early in the morning, before the sun was visible, Vasudeva came from the stable and went to his friend.

"You have not slept," he said.

"No, Vasudeva. I sat here, I listened to the river. It told me a lot, it filled me deeply with the salutary thought, with the thought of the oneness."

"You have experienced sorrow, Siddhartha, but I see that no sadness has entered your heart."

"No, dear friend, why should I be sad? I, who was rich and happy, have now become even richer and happier. I have been given my son."

"Your son is welcome to me too. But now, Siddhartha, let us get to work, there is a lot to do. Kamala has died on the same pallet where once my wife died. Let us also build Kamala's funeral pyre on the same hill where once I built my wife's funeral pyre."

While the boy slept on, they built the pyre.

The Son

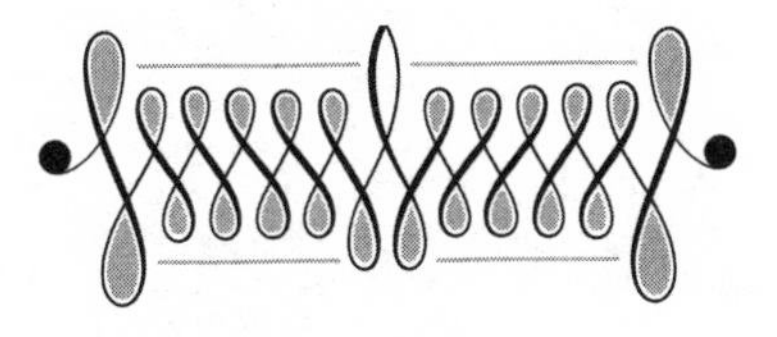

Timid and weeping, the boy had attended his mother's funeral; gloomy and timid, he had listened to Siddhartha, who had greeted him as his son and welcomed him in Vasudeva's hut. Pale he sat for days on the dead woman's hill, refused to eat, closed up his eyes, closed up his heart, strained and strove against destiny.

Siddhartha indulged him and let him be, he honored his grief. Siddhartha understood that his son did not know him, that he could not love him as a father. Slowly he saw and understood too that the eleven-year-old was a pampered boy, a mama's boy, brought up in the habits of wealth, accustomed to finer food, to a soft bed, accustomed to ordering servants around.

Siddhartha understood that the grieving, pampered boy could not suddenly and willingly be content in a strange place and in poverty. He did not force him, he did some chores for him, he always picked out the best morsel for him. He hoped he would win him over slowly, through friendly patience.

He had felt rich and happy when the boy had come to him. But time flowed on, and since the boy remained foreign and surly, displaying a proud and defiant heart, refusing to work, showing the old men no respect, robbing Vasudeva's fruit trees, Siddhartha began to realize that his son had brought not peace and happiness to him but sorrow and suffering. Still, he loved him, and he cherished the sorrow and suffering of love more than joy and happiness without the boy.

When young Siddhartha had arrived in the hut, the old men had divided their labor. Vasudeva had taken over as sole ferryman, and Siddhartha the labor in hut and field in order to be with his son.

For a long time, long months, Siddhartha waited for his son to understand, to accept his love, perhaps to love him back. For long months, Vasudeva waited, watched and waited and held his tongue. One evening, when the young Siddhartha had once again tortured his father with moods and defiance and had broken both the rice bowls, Vasudeva took his friend aside and spoke to him.

"Forgive me," he said, "but I am talking to you with a friendly heart. I see that you are in torment, I see that you are in anguish. Your son, dear friend, is causing you worry, and he is causing me worry too. The young bird is used to a different life, to a different nest. He did not flee the wealth and the town, as you did, out of disgust and surfeit; he had to leave them against his will. I have asked the river, my friend, I have asked it many times. But the river laughs, it laughs at me, it laughs at me and you, and it shakes with laughter at our folly. Water wants water, youth wants youth, your son is not in a place where he can thrive. You too ask the river, you too listen to its answer!"

Worried, Siddhartha gazed into the friendly face, its many wrinkles always wreathed in merriment.

"Can I part with him?" he asked softly, embarrassed. "Give me more time, dear friend! Look, I am fighting for him, I am wooing his heart, I want to capture it with love and friendly patience. Let the river speak to him too someday; he too is called."

Vasudeva's smile blossomed more warmly. "Oh,

yes, he too is called, he too is of eternal life. But do we know then, you and I, to what he is called, to what path, to what deeds, to what sufferings? His sufferings will not be small, his heart is too hard and proud. Such hearts must suffer much, wander much, do much injustice, saddle themselves with many sins. Tell me, dear friend: Are you not raising your son? Do you not force him? Do you not beat him? Do you not punish him?"

"No, Vasudeva, I do none of that."

"I knew it. You never force him, never beat him, never order him, because you know that soft is stronger than hard, water stronger than rock, love stronger than violence. Very good, I praise you. But is it not a mistake on your part to believe that you never force him, never punish him? Do you not bind him in bonds with your love? Do you not shame him daily and make things even harder for him with your kindness and patience? Do you not force him, the arrogant and pampered boy, to live in a hut with two old banana eaters, for whom even rice is a delicacy, whose thoughts cannot be his, whose hearts are old and silent and take a different course from his? Is he not forced by all this, not punished?"

Abashed, Siddhartha gazed at the ground. Softly he asked: "What do you think I should do?"

Vasudeva said: "Take him to town, take him to his mother's house. Some servants must still be there, put him in their care. And if none are left, then take him to a teacher, not for the teaching, but so that he can be with other boys, and with girls, and in the world that is his. Have you never thought of that?"

"You see into my heart," said Siddhartha sadly. "I have often thought of that. But look, he has no gentle heart—so how can I put him in that world? Will he not become haughty, will he not surrender to pleasure and power, will he not repeat all his father's mistakes, will he not perhaps lose himself entirely in samsara?"

The ferryman's smile beamed bright; he gently touched Siddhartha's arm and said: "Ask the river, my friend! Hear it laugh at that! Do you really believe you committed your follies to spare your son? And can you shield your son against samsara? How? Through teaching, through praying, through admonishing? My friend, have you fully forgotten that tale, that instructive tale you once told me here, about Siddhartha, the Brahmin's son? Who saved Siddhartha the samana from samsara, from sin, from greed, from folly? Could his father's piety, his teachers' admonitions, his own knowing, his own seeking, save him? What father, what teacher could shield him from living his own life, soiling himself with life, burdening himself with guilt, drinking the bitter drink himself, finding his path himself? Do you really believe, dear friend, that anyone at all is spared this path? Perhaps your little son because you love him, because you would like to spare him pain and sorrow and disillusion? But even if you died for him ten times over, you could not take away even the tiniest bit of his destiny."

Never had Vasudeva spoken so many words. Siddhartha thanked him in a friendly fashion, went, worried, into the hut, but found no sleep for a long time. Vasudeva had told him nothing that he himself had not already thought and known. But it was a knowledge he could not act on; stronger than his knowledge was his love for the boy, stronger his tenderness, his fear of losing him. Had he ever lost his heart so greatly, had he ever loved anyone like this, with a love so blind, so painful, so futile, and yet so happy?

Siddhartha could not take his friend's advice, he

could not give up his son. He let the boy order him around, he let him despise him. Silently he waited, daily he began the mute struggle of friendliness, the soundless war of patience. Vasudeva also silently waited, friendly, knowing, forbearing. In patience they were both masters.

Once, when the boy's face reminded him very much of Kamala, Siddhartha recalled something she had said to him long ago, in the days of youth. "You cannot love," she had said to him, and he had agreed with her, and had likened himself to a star and the child people to falling leaves, and yet he had sensed a rebuke in her words. Indeed, he had never been able to lose himself completely in anyone else, give himself completely to another person, forget himself, commit follies of love for someone else. He had never been able to do these things, and this had struck him as the great gap between him and the child people. But now that his son was here, now he, Siddhartha, too, had become a child person, suffering for someone else, loving someone else, lost in a love, a fool for love. Now he too, at this late time, felt this strongest and strangest passion, suffered from it, suffered woefully, and yet he was blissful, was somewhat renewed, was somewhat richer.

He did sense that this love, this blind love for his son, was a passion, something very human, that it was samsara, a troubled wellspring, a dark water. Yet he also felt that it was not worthless, that it was necessary, came from his own being. This pleasure too had to be atoned for, these pains too had to be savored, these follies too had to be committed.

Meanwhile the son let him commit his follies, let him woo, humiliated him daily with his moods. This father had nothing for the son to delight in and nothing to fear. He was a good man, this father, a good, a kind, a gentle man, perhaps a very pious man, perhaps a saint—but none of these were qualities that could win the boy over. He was bored with this father, who kept him captive in his wretched hut, he was bored with him and with his way of responding to every rotten act with smiles, to every insult with friendliness, to every nastiness with kindness—that was the most hateful cunning of that old conniver. The boy would much rather have been threatened by him, mistreated by him.

A day came when young Siddhartha blurted out his feelings and openly turned against his father. His father had given him a chore, had told him to gather brushwood. But the boy did not leave the hut, he stood there, defiant and furious, stamped his foot, clenched his fists, and, in violent eruption, yelled hate and scorn in his father's face.

"Get brushwood yourself!" he shouted, foaming, "I'm not your slave. I know you won't hit me, you don't dare. I know you constantly want to punish me and belittle me with your piety and your indulgence. You want me to be like you, just as pious, just as gentle, just as wise! But listen: to spite you, I'd rather be a highwayman and murderer and go to hell than become like you! I hate you, you're not my father, even if you were my mother's lover ten times over!"

Grief and anger boiled over in him, foamed toward the father in a hundred wild and evil words. Then the boy ran away and did not come back till late in the evening.

But the next morning he had disappeared. And also gone was a small woven basket of two-colored baste, where the ferryman kept the copper and silver coins they received as fares. And also gone was the boat. Siddhartha saw it lying on the opposite bank. The boy had run away.

"I have to follow him," said Siddhartha, who had been trembling since yesterday because of the boy's abusive words. "A child cannot go through the forest alone. He will die. We have to build a raft, Vasudeva, to cross the water."

"We will build a raft," said Vasudeva, "to get back our boat, which the boy has taken away. But as for him, dear friend, you should let him go. He's no longer a child, he can take care of himself. He is seeking the path to town, and he is right, do not forget that. He is doing what you yourself have failed to do. He is taking care of himself, he is going his own way. Ah, Siddhartha, I see you suffering, but you are suffering pains that others would laugh at, that you will soon laugh at yourself."

Siddhartha did not reply. He was already clutching the ax, and he began to make a raft of bamboo, and Vasudeva helped him to bind the canes with grass ropes. Then they rafted across, were carried far, pulled the raft upstream on the opposite bank.

"Why have you brought the ax along?" asked Siddhartha.

Vasudeva said: "An oar of our boat may have been lost."

But Siddhartha knew what his friend was thinking. He was thinking that the boy had thrown away or shattered the oar to avenge himself and to prevent them from following him. And indeed, no oar was left in the boat. Vasudeva pointed to the bottom of the boat and smiled at his friend as if to say: "Don't you see what your son is trying to tell you? Don't you see that he doesn't want to be followed?" But he did not put those thoughts into words. He set about making a new oar. Siddhartha, however, said good-bye and went to seek the runaway. Vasudeva did not hinder him.

After Siddhartha had been walking through the forest for a long time, it occurred to him that his seeking was useless. Either, he thought, the boy was far ahead of him and had already reached the town, or, if he was still on the way, he would hide from this man who was following him. Thinking further, he also found that he was no longer worried about his son; deep down he knew that his son neither had perished nor was menaced by any danger in the forest. Nevertheless he ran without resting, no longer to rescue his son; he desired only to see him perhaps. And he ran until he reached the town.

But when he came to the broad road near the town, he halted at the entrance to the beautiful pleasure garden that had once belonged to Kamala, where he had first seen her in her sedan. Again the bygone arose in his soul, again he saw himself standing there, a bearded, naked samana, his hair full of dust. For a long time Siddhartha stood there, peering through the open gate into the garden. He saw monks in yellow cowls wandering under the beautiful trees.

For a long time he stood, reflecting, seeing images, listening to the tale of his life. For a long time he stood, gazing at the monks, saw young Siddhartha instead of them, saw young Kamala walking under the tall trees. He clearly saw himself being regaled by Kamala, receiving her first kiss, proudly and scornfully looking back at his Brahmin years, proudly and yearningly beginning his worldly life. He saw Kamaswami, saw the servants, the banquets, the dicers, the musicians, saw Kamala's songbird in its cage, relived all these things, breathed samsara, was again old and tired, again felt the disgust, again felt the wish to snuff himself out, again was healed by the holy om.

After standing and standing at the garden gate, Siddhartha realized how foolish was the desire that had driven him to this place; he realized that he could not help his son, that he must not cling to him. He felt deep love in his heart for the runaway, it was like a wound; and he also felt that the wound was not for wallowing, that it must become a blossom and shine.

It saddened him that the wound was not yet blossoming, not yet radiant. The goal of his wish, which had drawn him here, after the runaway son, was now replaced by emptiness. Sad, he settled down, felt something dying in his heart, felt emptiness, saw no more joy, no goal. He sat there waiting, lost in thought. That was what he had learned on the river, that one thing: to wait, to listen, to have patience. And he sat and listened, in the dust of the street, listened to his sad and weary heart, waited for its voice. For several hours, he squatted there, listening, saw no more images, sank into emptiness, let himself sink, without seeing a way. And whenever he felt the burning wound, he soundlessly uttered the om, filled himself with om. The monks in the garden saw him, and since he squatted for many hours, with the dust collecting on his gray hair, one monk came over and placed two pisang fruits before him. The old man did not see him.

From this daze a hand awoke him, touching his shoulder. Instantly he recognized this touch, tender and timid, and he came to. He stood up and greeted Vasudeva, who had followed him. And peering into Vasudeva's friendly face, into the small wrinkles filled with smiling, into the cheerful eyes, he also smiled. He now saw the pisang fruits lying in front of him; he picked them up, gave one to the ferryman, and ate the other himself. Then he silently went back to the forest with Vasudeva, returned home to the ferry. Neither spoke about what had happened that day, neither uttered the boy's name, neither spoke about his escape, neither spoke about the wound. In the hut, Siddhartha lay down on his pallet, and when Vasudeva came over after a while to offer him a bowl of coconut milk, he found him asleep.

Om

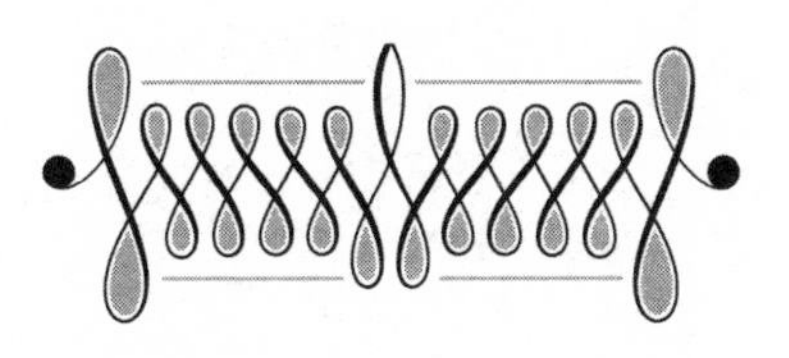

The wound burned for a long time. Siddhartha had to ferry many travelers who had a son or a daughter along, and he saw none of them without envying them, without thinking: "So many, so many thousands have this sweetest happiness—why not I? Even wicked people, even thieves and robbers, have children, and love them and are loved by them, but not I."

His thoughts were that simple, without understanding: he had grown that similar to the child people.

He now saw people in a different light, less cleverly, less proudly, but also more warmly, more curiously, more sympathetically. When he ferried normal travelers, child people, businessmen, warriors, women, they no longer seemed foreign to him. He understood them, he understood and shared their lives, which were led not by thoughts and insights, but solely by drives and wishes. And he felt like them. Although he was close to perfection, and enduring his final wound, he saw these child people as his brothers. Their greed, their vanity, their silliness had lost their silliness for him, became understandable, became lovable, became even venerable for him. A mother's blind love for her child, a conceited father's blind and stupid love for his only little son, a vain young woman's blind, wild striving for jewelry and worshipful male eyes—all these urges, all these childish feelings, all these simple, foolish, yet tremendously potent, powerfully living, powerfully triumphant drives and desires were no longer infantile for Siddhartha. He saw people living for their sake, saw them achieving endless things for their sake, traveling, waging wars, suffering endlessly, enduring endlessly, and he could love them for that; he saw life, liveliness, indestructibility, Brahma in each of their passions, each of their deeds. Lovable and admirable were these people in their blind devotion, their blind strength and tenacity. They lacked nothing, the knower and thinker had nothing over them but a single trifle, a single tiny little thing: the consciousness, the conscious thought of the oneness of all life. And at times, Siddhartha even doubted whether this knowing, this thinking were so valuable, whether they were not childish things of the thought people, the thought-child-people. In all other respects, the worldlings were the equals of the sage, were often far superior, just as at times, animals, in their tenacious, unswerving, necessary actions, may seem superior to human beings.

Slowly blossomed, slowly ripened in Siddhartha the insight, the knowledge of what wisdom actually is, what the goal of his long seeking was. It was nothing but a readiness of the soul, an ability, a secret art, to think the thought of oneness, to feel and breathe the oneness at every moment, in the midst of life. Slowly this blossomed in him, brightly emanated to him from Vasudeva's old childlike face: harmony, knowledge of the eternal perfection of the world, smiling, oneness.

But the wound still burned; bitterly Siddhartha thought about his son, yearned for him, nurtured his love and tenderness in his heart, let the pain devour him, committed all the follies of love. This flame did not die of its own accord.

And one day, when the wound was burning fiercely, Siddhartha, driven by longing, ferried across the river, disembarked, and wanted to go to town and seek his son. The river flowed softly and gently, it was the dry season of the year, but the river's voice sounded strange. It was laughing! It was clearly laughing. The river was laughing, it laughed, clear and bright, at the old ferryman. Siddhartha halted, he leaned over the water the better to hear, and in the silently flowing water he saw his own face reflected, and in this reflected face there was something that reminded him, something forgotten, and by pondering it, he found it. This face resembled another face, that he had once known and loved and also feared. It resembled the face of his father, the Brahmin. And he remembered that ages ago, he, a youth, had forced his father to let him join the penitents, he remembered saying good-bye to him, going away, and never returning. Had not his father suffered the same sorrow that Siddhartha was now suffering for his own son? Had his father not died long since, alone, without seeing his son again? Would Siddhartha not have to suffer the same fate? Was it not a comedy, a strange and stupid thing, this repetition, this running in a fateful circle?

The river laughed. Yes, it was so. Everything not fully suffered, not fully resolved came again: the same sorrows were suffered over and over.

Siddhartha stepped back into the boat and rowed back to the hut, recalling his father, recalling his son, laughed to scorn by the river, at odds with himself, inclined toward despair and inclined no less to join the loud laughter at himself and the whole world. Ah, the wound was not blossoming yet, his heart was still defying fate, serenity and victory were not yet beaming from his sorrow. Still, he felt hope, and upon returning to the hut, he had an invincible desire to open up to Vasudeva, to disclose everything to him, reveal everything to him, the master of listening.

Vasudeva was sitting in the hut, weaving a basket. He no longer worked the ferry, his eyes were starting to weaken, and not only his eyes, but also his arms and his hands. Unaltered and blossoming were only the joy and the serene benevolence of his face.

Siddhartha sat down with the old man; slowly he began to speak. He now talked about things they had never spoken of before: about his trip to the town back then, about the burning wound, about his envy at the sight of happy fathers, about his knowledge of the folly of such feelings, about his futile struggle against them. He reported everything, he could say everything, even the most embarrassing things—everything could be said, everything told, everything disclosed. He showed his wound and told about his flight today: about crossing the water, a childish fleer, willing to walk to town, and he told about the river's laughing.

As he spoke, on and on, and Vasudeva listened with a silent face, Siddhartha felt Vasudeva's listening, felt it more intensely than ever before; he felt his own pains and anxieties flowing across to him, his secret hope flowing across and coming back. Revealing his wound to this listener was the same as bathing it in the river until it grew cool and was one with the river. Still speaking, still admitting and confessing, Siddhartha felt more and more that this was no longer Vasudeva, no longer a human being, listening to him, that this motionless listener was absorbing his confession like a tree absorbing rain, that this motionless man was the river itself, that he was God himself, that he was eternity itself. And while Siddhartha stopped thinking about himself and his wound, this knowledge of Vasudeva's altered being took possession of him, and the more he felt it and pierced it, the less peculiar it became, the more he realized that everything was right and natural, that Vasudeva had been like that for a long time, nearly always, but that he, Siddhartha, had not fully recognized it, and that he himself was barely different from Vasudeva. He felt that he now saw old Vasudeva the way the populace sees the gods, and that this could not last. He began to say farewell to Vasudeva in his heart. And he kept speaking all the while.

When Siddhartha was finished speaking, Vasudeva gazed at him with his friendly, somewhat weakened eyes, said nothing, silently radiated love and serenity toward him, understanding and knowledge. He took Siddhartha's hand, led him to the seat on the riverbank, sat down with him, smiled at the river.

"You heard it laugh," said Vasudeva. "But you have not heard everything. Let us listen, you will hear more."

They listened. The many-voiced song of the river resounded softly. Siddhartha stared into the water, and images appeared to him in the flow: his father appeared, lonely, mourning his son; he himself, Siddhartha, appeared, lonely, he too bound with the bonds of yearning for his faraway son; his son appeared, lonely he too, the boy, greedily charging along on the burning path of his young wishes: each person focusing on his goal, each one obsessed with his goal, each one suffering. The river sang with a sorrowful voice, sang ardently, flowed ardently toward its goal, its voice lamenting.

"Do you hear?" asked Vasudeva's mute gaze. Siddhartha nodded.

"Hear better!" whispered Vasudeva.

Siddhartha strove to hear better. His father's image, his own image, his son's image flowed in and out of one another. Kamala's image also appeared and dissolved, and Govinda's image and other images flowed into one another. They all merged into the flow, they all flowed as a river toward the goal, ardent, desiring, suffering; and the river's voice was full of yearning, full of burning distress, full of insatiable longing. The river flowed toward the goal; Siddhartha saw it hastening—the river consisting of him and his near and dear and all the people he had ever seen; all the waves and the waters hastened, suffering, toward goals, many goals; the waterfall, the lake, the rapids, the sea, and all goals were attained; and each goal was followed by another, and the water became vapor and rose to the sky, became rain and plunged down from the sky, became a source, became a brook, became a river, strove anew, flowed anew. But the ardent voice had changed. It still resounded, sorrowful, seeking, but other voices joined in, voices of joy and sorrow, good and evil voices, laughing and grieving, a hundred voices, a thousand voices.

Siddhartha listened. He was now all ears, utterly engrossed in listening, utterly empty, utterly absorbing. He felt he had now learned all there was to know about listening. He had often heard all these things, these many voices in the river, but today it all sounded new. He could no longer distinguish the many voices, the cheerful from the weeping, the children's from the men's: they all belonged together. The lament of the knower's yearning and laughing, the screaming of the angry, the moaning of the dying—everything was one, everything was entwined and entwisted, was interwoven a thousandfold. And all of it together, all voices, all goals, all yearnings, all sufferings, all pleasures, all good and evil—the world was everything together. Everything together was the river of events, was the music of life. And when Siddhartha listened attentively to this river, listened to this song of a thousand voices, when he did not listen to sorrow or laughter, when he did not bind his soul to any one voice and did not enter them with his ego, but listened to all of them, heard the wholeness, the oneness—then the great song of the thousand voices consisted of a single word, which was "om": perfection.

"Do you hear?" Vasudeva's eyes asked again.

Radiant was Vasudeva's smile, it hovered, luminous, over all the wrinkles in his old face just as the om hovered over all the voices of the river. Bright shone his smile when he looked at his friend, and bright now glowed the very same smile on Siddhartha's face. His wound blossomed, his sorrow was radiant, his ego had flowed into the oneness.

At that moment Siddhartha stopped fighting with destiny, stopped suffering. On his face the serenity of knowledge blossomed, knowledge that no will can resist, that knows perfection, that agrees with the flow of events, with the river of life, full of compassion, full of shared pleasure, devoted to the flowing, belonging to the oneness.

When Vasudeva rose from his seat on the riverbank, when he looked into Siddhartha's eyes and saw the radiant serenity of knowledge, he touched Siddhartha's shoulder lightly, in his cautious and tender way, and said: "I have waited for this moment, dear friend. Now it has come; let me go. I have waited and waited for this moment, I was Vasudeva the ferryman for years and years. Now it is enough. Farewell, hut, farewell, river, farewell, Siddhartha!"

Siddhartha bowed low to the departing man.

"I knew it," he murmured. "Will you go into the forest?"

"I am going into the forest, I am going into the oneness," said Vasudeva, radiant.

Radiant, he went away; Siddhartha gazed after him. Deeply joyous, deeply earnest, he gazed after him, saw his steps full of peace, saw his head full of radiance, saw his figure full of light.

Govinda

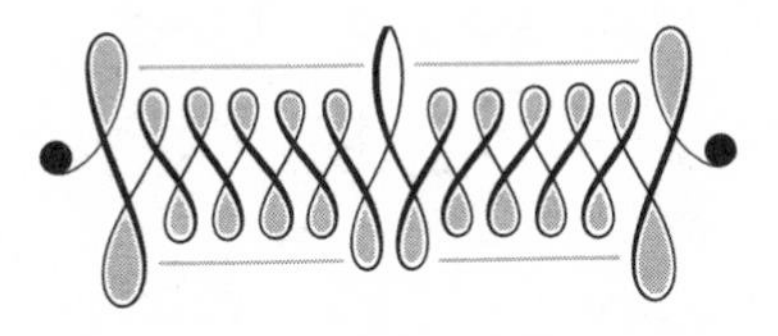

Once, during a rest period, Govinda was with other monks in the pleasure grove that the courtesan Kamala had given to Gautama's disciples. Govinda heard them talk about an old ferryman who lived on the river, a day's journey from here, and who was viewed by many as a sage. When Govinda wandered on, he chose the way to the ferry, eager to see this ferryman. For though Govinda had lived all his life according to the Rule and was also revered by the young monks for his age and his modesty, the disquiet and seeking were not snuffed in his heart.

He came to the river, he asked the old man to ferry him across, and when they got out on the other side, he said to the old man: "You show much goodness to us monks and pilgrims, you have ferried many of us across. Are not you too, ferryman, a seeker of the right path?"

Siddhartha, smiling with his old eyes, said: "Do you call yourself a seeker, O Venerable One, and yet you are well on in years and you wear the robe of Gautama's monks?"

"It is true, I am old," said Govinda, "but I have not stopped seeking. Never will I stop seeking—this seems to be my destiny. You too, it seems to me, have sought. Will you say a word to me, Honored One?"

Siddhartha said: "What could I say to you, Venerable One? Perhaps that you are seeking too hard? That you seek so hard that you do not find?"

"What do you mean?" asked Govinda.

"When someone seeks," said Siddhartha, "then it easily happens that his eyes see only the thing that he seeks, and he is able to find nothing, to take in nothing because he always thinks only about the thing he is seeking, because he has one goal, because he is obsessed with his goal. Seeking means: having a goal. But finding means: being free, being open, having no goal. You, Venerable One, may truly be a seeker, for, in striving toward your goal, you fail to see certain things that are right under your nose."

"I do not yet fully understand," said Govinda. "What do you mean by that?"

Siddhartha said: "Once, O Venerable One, years ago, you were already on this river and you saw a sleeper by the river, and you sat with him to guard his sleep. But, O Govinda, you did not recognize the sleeper."

Amazed, virtually spellbound, the monk looked into the ferryman's eyes.

"Are you Siddhartha?" he asked in a shy voice. "I wouldn't have recognized you this time either! I heartily greet you, Siddhartha, I am heartily delighted to see you again! You've changed greatly, my friend. And so now you've become a ferryman?"

Siddhartha laughed in a friendly fashion. "A ferryman, yes. Some people, Govinda, must change greatly, must wear all kinds of clothes; and I am one of those people, dear friend. Welcome, Govinda, and please spend the night in my hut."

Govinda spent the night in the hut and slept on the pallet that had once been Vasudeva's pallet. He asked the friend of his youth many questions; Siddhartha had to tell him a lot about his life.

The next morning, when it was time to begin his day's wandering, Govinda, not without hesitating, spoke these words: "Before I continue on my way, Siddhartha, permit me one last question. Do you have a teaching? Do you have a faith or a knowledge that you follow, that helps you live and do right?"

Siddhartha said: "You know, dear friend, as a young man, back then, when we lived with the penitents in the forest, I already came to distrust the teachings and the teachers and I turned my back on them. Nor have I changed in that regard. Nevertheless I have had many teachers since then. For a long time a beautiful courtesan was my teacher, and a rich merchant was my teacher, and so were several dicers. Once, a wandering disciple of the Buddha was my teacher; he sat with me during his pilgrimage when I had fallen asleep in the forest. I learned from him too, I was thankful to him too, very thankful. But most of all I have learned from this river and from my forerunner, Vasudeva the ferryman. He was a very simple person, Vasudeva, he was no thinker, but he knew what was essential as well as Gautama did: he was a perfect man, a saint."

Govinda said: "Oh, Siddhartha, you still seem to like joking a bit. I believe you and I know that you have not followed any teacher. But have you not found, if not a teaching, then certain thoughts, certain insights that are your own and that help you live? If you told me a little about them, you would delight my heart."

Siddhartha said: "I have had thoughts, yes, and insights, now and then. Sometimes, for an hour or for a day, I have felt knowledge in me the way we feel life in our hearts. There were a number of thoughts, but it would be hard for me to communicate them to you. Listen, my Govinda, this is one of my thoughts that I have found: Wisdom cannot be communicated. Wisdom that a wise man tries to communicate always sounds foolish."

"Are you joking?" asked Govinda.

"I am not joking. I am telling you what I have found. Knowledge can be communicated, but not wisdom. We can find it, we can live it, we can be carried by it, we can work wonders with it, but we cannot utter it or teach it. That was what I sometimes sensed in my youth, what drove me away from the teachers. I have found a thought, Govinda, that you will again take as a joke or as folly, but it is my best thought. This is it: The opposite of every truth is just as true! You see: A truth can be uttered and clad in words only if it is one-sided. One-sided is everything that can be thought with thoughts and said in words—

everything one-sided, everything half, everything is devoid of wholeness, of roundness, of oneness. When the sublime Gautama spoke and taught about the world, he had to divide it into samsara and Nirvana, into illusion and truth, into sorrow and salvation. There is no other choice, there is no other way for the man who wishes to teach. But the world itself, the Being around us and within us, is never one-sided. Never is a man or a deed all samsara or all Nirvana, never is a man all saintly or all sinful. It seems otherwise because we are prey to the illusion that time is a reality. But time is not real, Govinda; I have experienced this time and time again. And if time is not real, then the span that seems to lie between world and eternity, between sorrow and bliss, between evil and good is also an illusion."

"What do you mean?" asked Govinda uneasily.

"Listen well, dear friend, listen well! The sinner that I am and that you are is a sinner, but someday he will be a Brahmin again, someday he will achieve Nirvana, he will be a Buddha. And now listen: This 'someday' is an illusion, is merely a metaphor! The sinner is not on the way to becoming a Buddha, he is not involved in a development, although our thinking cannot imagine things in any other way. No, the sinner now and today, already contains the future Buddha, his future is fully here; you must worship in the sinner, in you, in everyone, the developing, the possible, the hidden Buddha. The world, my friend, Govinda, is not imperfect or developing slowly toward perfection. No, the world is perfect at every moment, all sin already contains grace, all youngsters already contain oldsters, all babies contain death, all the dying contain eternal life. It is not possible for any man to see how far along another man is on his way; Buddha is waiting in robbers and dicers, the robber is waiting in the Brahmin. In deep meditation it is possible to eliminate time, to see all past, all present, all developing life as coexisting, and everything is good, everything perfect, everything is Brahma. This is why that which is seems good to me, death seems like life, sin seems like saintliness, cleverness like foolishness, everything must be like that, everything needs only my assent, only my willingness, my loving agreement; it is good for me like that, it can never harm me. In my body and in my soul I realized that I greatly needed sin, I needed lust, vanity, the striving for goods, and I needed the most shameful despair to learn how to give up resistance, to learn how to love the world, to stop comparing the world with any world that I wish for, that I imagine, with any perfection that I think up; I learned how to let the world be as it is, and to love it and to belong to it gladly. Those, O Govinda, are some of the thoughts that have crossed my mind."

Siddhartha bent down, picked up a stone, and weighed it in his hand.

"This here," he said playfully, "is a stone, and perhaps at a certain time it will be soil and will, from soil, become a plant, or an animal or a human being. Now earlier I would have said: 'This stone is merely a stone, it is worthless, it belongs to the world of maya. But since in the cycle of transmutations it can also become a man and mind, I grant worth to this stone too.' That was what I might have thought earlier. But today I think: 'This stone is a stone, it is also an animal, it is also God, it is also the Buddha, I love and honor it not because it could become this or that someday, but because it is everything long since and always—and it is precisely because of this, because it is a stone, because it appears to me now and today as a stone, it is precisely because of this that I love it and see worth and meaning in each of its veins and pits, in the yellow, in the gray, in the hardness, in the sound it emits when I tap it, in the dryness or dampness of its surface.' There are stones that feel like oil or like soap, and others like leaves, still others like sand, and each is special and prays the om in its own way, each is Brahma; but at the same time and just as much it is a stone, is oily or soapy, and that is precisely what I like and what seems wonderful to me and worthy of worship."

"But I will say no more about it. Words are not good for the secret meaning, everything instantly becomes a bit different when we utter it, a bit adulterated, a bit foolish—yes, and that too is very good and appeals to me, I also very much agree that one man's treasure and wisdom always sound like foolishness to another."

Govinda listened in silence.

"Why did you tell me about the stone?" he hesitantly asked after a pause.

"It was unintentional. Or perhaps I meant that I love the stone and the river and all these things that we contemplate and from which we can learn. I can love a stone, Govinda, and also a tree or a piece of bark. These are things, and things can be loved. But I cannot love words. That is why teachings mean nothing to me, they have no hardness, no softness, no colors, no edges, no smell, no taste, they have nothing but words. Perhaps that is what keeps you from finding peace, perhaps it is the many words. For redemption and virtue, samsara and Nirvana are also mere words, Govinda. There is no thing that is Nirvana; there is only the word 'Nirvana.'"

Govinda said: "Nirvana, my friend, is not only a word. It is also a thought."

Siddhartha went on: "A thought—that may be. I must confess to you, dear friend: I barely distinguish between thoughts and words. Frankly, I have little esteem for thoughts. I have more esteem for things. Here on this ferry, for example, there was a man, my forerunner and teacher, a saintly man; for years he simply believed in the river, and in nothing else. He noticed that the river's voice spoke to him; he learned from its voice, it raised him and taught him. The river seemed like a god to him. For many years he did not know that every wind, every cloud, every bird, every bug is just as godly and knows and can teach just as much as the venerated river. But when this saint went into the forest, he knew everything, knew more than you and I, without teachers, without books, only because he believed in the river."

Govinda said: "But is what you call 'things' something real, something essential? Are they too not a mirage of the maya, merely image and semblance? Your stone, your tree, your river—are they realities?"

"This too," said Siddhartha, "does not trouble me greatly. Whether things are semblances or not, I too am a semblance, after all, and so they are always my peers. That is what makes them so dear to me and venerable: they are my peers. That is why I can love them. And now this is a teaching that you will laugh at: Love, O Govinda, seems paramount to me. Seeing through the world, explaining it, despising it may be crucial to great thinkers. But all I care about is to be able to love the world, not to despise it, not to hate it or myself, to be able to view it and myself and all beings with love and admiration and awe."

"I understand that," said Govinda. "But that was the very thing that he, the Sublime One, recognized as mirage. He taught benevolence, indulgence, compassion, tolerance, but not love: he forbade us to fetter our hearts in love for anything earthly."

"I know," said Siddhartha; his smile beamed golden. "I know, Govinda. And look, here we are in the midst of the thicket of opinions, in the fight over words. For I cannot deny that my words about love contradict, seem to contradict, Gautama's words. That is precisely why I so greatly distrust words, for I know that this contradiction is an illusion. I know that I am one with Gautama. How could he then not also know love? He, who recognized all humanness in its ephemeralness, in its vanity, and yet loved human beings so much that he devoted a long and arduous life purely to helping them, to teaching them! Even with him, even with this great teacher, the things are dearer to me than words, his life and deeds more important than his speaking, the gestures of his hands more important than his opinions. I see his greatness not in speaking, not in thinking, but only in doing, in living."

For a long time the two old men kept silent. Then Govinda spoke as he bowed before departing: "I thank you, Siddhartha, for telling me something of your thoughts. Some of your thoughts are strange, I did not understand all of them right away. Be that as it may, I thank you and I wish you peaceful days."

But secretly he thought: This Siddhartha is a peculiar person, he utters peculiar thoughts, his teaching sounds foolish. The pure Teaching of the Sublime One sounds different, sounds clearer, purer, more intelligible; there is nothing strange, foolish, or laughable about it. However, Siddhartha's hands and feet, his eyes, his brow, his breathing, his smile, his greeting, his gait seem different from his thoughts. Never since our sublime Gautama entered Nirvana, never have I met another man about whom I felt: This is a saint! I have felt this way only about him, this Siddhartha. His teaching may be strange, his words may sound foolish, but his eyes and his hands, his skin and his hair—everything about him radiates a purity, radiates a peace, radiates a mildness and serenity and saintliness, which I have seen in no other person since the final death of our sublime teacher.

With these thoughts and a conflict in his heart, Govinda bowed once more to Siddhartha, drawn by love. Deeply he bowed to the peaceful sitter.

"Siddhartha," he said, "we are old men now. We will scarcely meet again in this incarnation. I see, dear friend, that you have found peace. I confess that I have not found it. Give me, my honored friend, another word, give me something that I can grasp, that I can understand! Give me something to take along on my way. My way is often arduous, it is often dark, Siddhartha."

Siddhartha silently looked at him with his still and unchanging smile. Govinda stared into Siddhartha's face with fear, with yearning. Sorrow and eternal seeking were written in his gaze, eternal failure to find.

Siddhartha saw it and smiled.

"Lean toward me!" he whispered in Govinda's ear. "Lean toward me here! Right, a bit closer! Very close! Kiss my forehead, Govinda!"

But while Govinda, surprised and yet drawn by great love and premonition, obeyed Siddhartha's words, leaned over to him, and touched his forehead with his lips, something wonderful happened to him. While his thoughts still dwelled on Siddhartha's peculiar words, while he vainly and reluctantly tried to think time away, to imagine Nirvana and samsara as one, while a certain scorn for his friend's words struggled in him with tremendous love and reverence, this happened to him:

He no longer saw his friend Siddhartha's face; instead he saw other faces, many, a long row, a streaming river of faces, hundreds, thousands, which all came and faded, and yet seemed all to be there at once, which kept changing and being renewed, and yet which all were Siddhartha. He saw the face of a fish, a carp, with a mouth open in infinite pain, a dying fish, with breaking eyes—he saw the face of a newborn child, red and wrinkled, twisted with weeping—he saw the face of a murderer, saw him plunge a knife in another man's body—he saw, in the same second, this criminal chained and kneeling and his head chopped off by a stroke of the executioner's ax—he saw the naked bodies of men and women in positions and struggles of raging love—he saw corpses stretched out, still, cold, empty—he saw the heads of animals, of boars, of crocodiles, of elephants, of bulls, of birds—he saw gods, saw Krishna, saw Agni—he saw all these shapes and faces in a thousand interrelations, each helping the others, loving them, hating them, destroying them, bearing them anew. Each was a desire to die, a passionately painful confession of ephemeralness, and yet none died, each was merely transformed, kept being reborn, kept receiving a new face, with no time between one face and the other—and all these shapes and faces rested, flowed, produced themselves and one another, floated away and poured into one another, and yet drawn over all of them there was constantly something thin, something unsubstantial, yet existing, like thin glass or ice, like a transparent skin, a shell or form or mask of water, and this mask smiled, and this mask was Siddhartha's smiling face, that he,

Govinda, touched with his lips at that very same moment. And Govinda saw that this smile of the mask, this smile of the oneness over the streaming formations, this smile of simultaneity over the thousand births and deaths, this smile of Siddhartha's was exactly the same, was exactly the identical still, fine, impenetrable, perhaps kindly, perhaps quizzical, wise, thousandfold smile of Gautama, the Buddha, as he himself, Govinda, had seen it with awe a hundred times. This, Govinda knew, was how the Perfect Ones smiled.

No longer knowing whether time existed, whether this seeing had lasted a second or a century, no longer knowing whether a Siddhartha existed, or a Gautama, or I and Thou, wounded in his innermost as if by a godly arrow, whose wounding tasted sweet, enchanted and dissolved in his innermost, Govinda stood for a brief while, leaning over Siddhartha's silent face, which he had just kissed, which had just been the setting of all formations, all Becoming, all Being. The face was unaltered after the depth of the thousandfold forms had closed again under its surface. He was still smiling, smiling softly and quietly, perhaps very gently, perhaps very mockingly—just as *he* had smiled, the Sublime One.

Govinda bowed low. Tears ran over his old face, but he was unaware of them; the feeling of deepest love, of humblest veneration burned in his heart like a fire. He bowed low, down to the ground, bowed to the motionless sitter, whose smile reminded him of everything that he had ever loved in his life, that had ever been valuable and holy to him in his life.